RAVEN
FINDS THE
DAYLIGHT
and other American Indian Stories

Paul M. Levitt & Elissa S. Guralnick

Illustrated by Carolynn Roche

RAVEN
FINDS THE
DAYLIGHT

and other

American
Indian Stories

Paul M. Levitt

& Elissa S. Guralnick

Illustrated by Carolynn Roche

CLEAR LIGHT PUBLISHING
SANTA FE, NEW MEXICO
www.clearlightbooks.com

© 2012 Paul M. Levitt, Elissa S. Guralnick, and illustrator Carolynn Roche
Clear Light Publishers, 823 Don Diego, Santa Fe, New Mexico 87505
www.clearlightbooks.com

FIRST EDITION
10 9 8 7 6 5 4 3 2 1

Library of Congress Cataloging-in-Publication Data

Levitt, Paul M.
[Stolen Appaloosa and other Indian Stories]
Raven Finds the Daylight and other American Indian Stories / Paul M. Levitt & Elissa S. Guralnick;
illustrated by Carolynn Roche.
— 1st ed.
   p. cm.
"These stories are taken, for the most part, from tales told by Indian tribes of the Pacific Northwest
and collected by the anthropologist Franz Boas"—T.p. verso.
ISBN-13: 978-1-57416-100-7
ISBN-10: 1-57416-100-8
1. Indians of North America—Northwest, Pacific—Folklore. 2. Indians of North America—Northwest Coast of
North America—Folklore. 3. Tales—Northwest, Pacific. 4. Tales—Northwest Coast of North America.
I. Guralnick, Elissa S. II. Roche, Carolynn, ill.
III. Boas, Franz, 1858-1942. IV. Title.

E78.N77L44 2011
398.209795—dc22
                    2010038191

DEDICATION

To our fathers, who told us fabulous stories of magic and monsters.

ACKNOWLEDGMENT

These stories are taken, for the most part, from tales told by Indian tribes
of the Pacific Northwest and collected by the anthropologist Franz Boas.
In the original manuscripts, the tales are often incomplete and fragmentary.
Hence, the authors have taken the liberty of building on their sources.
Nevertheless, to the rich and fertile minds of the First Americans,
we owe a great debt.

CONTENTS

The Bush-Tailed Rat Man

Bush-Tailed Rat Man, prowling through the night,
Making hardly any sound,
Keeping out of sight,
Stealing people's children, stealing people's food,
Bush-Tailed Rat Man,
You're too shrewd.

So sang Wayfarer, the wandering man, as he limped along a forest path near the banks of the Thompson River. Swish went his poor, lame foot through the leaves. Crackle went the forest twigs that snapped beneath his other foot, the good one. Years ago, as a child, he had broken his ankle; and because the bones were badly set, he had walked with a limp ever after. The limp made him slow, and also loud. Other Indians moved through the forest with light, quiet footsteps. But Wayfarer dragged along noisily, scaring off the animals and birds. Without anyone to keep him company or cheer him on his way, he sang himself a song that he had made up on his own.

Bush-Tailed Rat Man, hiding from the moon,
Not a star to light your way
To my storage room,
Taking what you fancy, taking what is mine,
Bush-Tailed Rat Man,
You're unkind.

Wayfarer's voice rang through the trees. It carried on the air right down to the banks of the river, where some Indian men from a nearby village were fishing.

"I hear a song," said the tall one.

"Something about the Bush-Tailed Rat Man," said the handsome one.

"Something about a thief," said the sad one.

Then they all fell silent and listened.

Bush-Tailed Rat Man, sneaking far away,
Bearing with you things you took,
For which you didn't pay,
Bring me back my children, bring me back my food.
Bush-Tailed Rat Man,
You're no good.

"Who do you suppose is singing?" asked the tall fisherman.

"Do you think what he's singing is true?" asked the handsome one.

"I don't know, but we ought to find out," said the sad one.

And with that, the, fishermen left their traps and went running through the forest to track down the singer. It didn't take them long to find him. His voice and his footsteps made it clear where he was, and his limp made him easy to catch up with.

"Whoa, there!" cried the fishermen. "Stop a minute, won't you?"

"Well, it all depends on what you want," said Wayfarer. "If you mean to make fun of my limp or to laugh at my song, I'd just as soon travel on. I've never understood why people wish to be rude, but often they insult a lonely wanderer, who wouldn't do them any harm."

"Look here, don't think we want to hurt you," said the tall fisherman. "All we had in mind was to ask about the song that you were singing. Is it true, what you said about the Bush-Tailed Rat Man?"

"And why should you want to know?" asked Wayfarer, still thinking that maybe these strangers were up to no good.

"Because not long ago," said the handsome one, "the Bush-Tailed Rat Man made his home in a cave among the rocks near our village. And ever since he came, food has been missing from our underground cellars."

"And your children?" asked Wayfarer. "What about your children?"

The sad fisherman bowed his head and wrung his hands, while the others clapped him on the shoulder to comfort him.

"His daughter," they explained, "she disappeared … and she was not the only child to vanish."

"Oh, woe is me," said Wayfarer. "This is the work of the Bush-Tailed Rat Man as sure as I am lame. He did the same to my people, and there is no way you can stop him from his stealing. When my people learned he was a thief, they tried to get back what he'd stolen. But the Bush-Tailed Rat Man outsmarted them all and destroyed my whole village."

"Tell us," said the fishermen; and right there on the forest path, they all sat down upon the ground to hear Wayfarer's tale.

"It happened like this," said Wayfarer. "For years the Bush-Tailed Rat Man lived in a cave not far from my people in a house made of rocks. Sometimes he would let us come to visit him, and we noticed that the door leading into his cave would open and close at his command. 'Spring open,' he would call, and the door would obey. 'Snap shut,' he would say, and the door would draw back. The children especially admired this trick and would come to see the magic door."

"Yes, it is the same with us," the fishermen observed.

"You must keep the children far away," said Wayfarer. "He lures them in and never lets them out."

"I should have warned her," said the father of the girl who had been stolen.

"But how?" said Wayfarer, hoping to console him. "How could you have warned your daughter when you didn't know yourself about the Bush-Tailed Rat Man's thieving? The people of my village lived for years without suspecting that he robbed them—although, I do admit, it struck us very strange that he sometimes served us heaping plates of food when we would visit. We never saw him hunt or fish, or gather berries, or dig for roots; and yet he always had an overflowing storeroom. Where did it come from?

"When we asked him, he insisted that his body was too weak to work. He said the Long-Tailed Mouse, his brother, gave him what he had—which he claimed was almost nothing. But even though we wanted to believe him, his story seemed impossible. What the Bush-Tailed Rat Man described as 'almost nothing' seemed to us a lot more food than we had. As for the Long-Tailed Mouse—why, that weakling couldn't have collected so much food in a thousand years. The longer we lived near the Bush-Tailed Rat Man, the more we were sure that he lied.

"Finally, one winter, we noticed that the cellars where we kept our food were being raided more than usual; and hoping to discover who was robbing us, a few of us kept watch for several nights. At first we saw nothing. But then, on an evening when the clouds covered up both the stars and the moon so that everything lay in deepest shadow, who should come sneaking to our cellars but the Bush-Tailed Rat Man! Silently, we watched him. Although we had but little light, we could see him gather up more food than he could carry. Then, making a pile of the things that he wanted, he hurried off to fetch his wife, so that she could help him bear away his treasure."

"Did you say wife?!" interrupted the fishermen. "We didn't know he had a wife!"

"Just wait, and you'll hear what became of her," said Wayfarer. "The very next morning, when everyone had woken, those of us who had been standing watch explained to all the others how the Bush-Tailed Rat Man tricked us. The villagers were angry and hurried off together to the Rat Man's cave to seize him. But because I'm lame and cannot run, I fell so far behind the group that everyone arrived before me.

"Now the Bush-Tailed Rat Man saw us coming and commanded his door to spring open. All of those in front of me hurried inside, whereupon the Rat Man cried, 'Snap shut!' and the door to his house closed tight, with me locked out. I beat on the door, but no one heard me. Finally, exhausted, I found an opening between two rocks and peeked through the crack to see what I could see inside his house.

"What a sight! The people appeared to be shouting at the Rat Man, though I couldn't hear their voices; and to judge from his face, I could see that he answered them rudely. They argued so long that I doubted they would ever stop. Then, suddenly, out of a room hidden off to the side, burst the children who'd been missing from the village! The villagers were overcome with joy, at least at first. But when they realized that the children had been stolen by the Rat Man, they grew terribly angry.

Enraged, they tried to grab him; but by dashing up and down the walls, he managed to escape their grasp, while his wife, in terror, cowered in the corner. So quickly did the Rat Man run, round and round the cave's thick walls and even straight across its ceiling, that the villagers grew dizzy as they watched him. So when suddenly he called for the cave door to open, in their dizziness they tripped and couldn't follow, as out he rushed and cried, 'Snap shut!' The door obeyed and not one of my people was able to escape.

"He didn't see me standing there. He didn't guess that I was watching while outside the cave he muttered magic words that made the rocks fall in upon the people, killing everyone inside, including his own wife. The beast! He never shed a tear for her. He merely laughed to see the harm he'd caused and went his way without regret. And now I see that this is where he came to, and that here, as well, he's doing harm."

Thus Wayfarer ended his story. There was nothing more to say. He was afraid to look into the eyes of the fishermen, because he didn't want to see their tears or have to hide his own.

For a long time, they were silent. Then one of the fishermen rose and remarked, "The sun is sinking fast behind the mountains to the west. Let us return to our village and tell the other people what we've heard."

"Yes," said his friends, as they stood and shook the forest dust from off their leggings. Then, turning to Wayfarer, they said, "We would be pleased if you would come with us and tell the tale yourself."

"I cannot follow fast," he said.

"Then we shall travel slowly," they replied. And together the four of them passed through the forest toward the village, three of them moving without any sound, and the fourth going swish with his bad foot and breaking forest twigs beneath his good one.

The villagers were glad to see the fishermen, who'd been gone so long that a scout had been sent to learn if they were having trouble with their traps. Finding no one there beside the river, the scout had emptied all the traps himself and brought back many fish, which now were being cooked upon the fire. So a dinner of fresh salmon awaited Wayfarer, who ate his fill, then told his tale again beside the fire while all the village listened.

No sooner had Wayfarer finished than the villagers leapt to their feet, intending to rush to the cave of the Rat Man and punish him for all his wicked ways. They grabbed their spears and hatchets and all but started up the path, when a powerful voice stopped them short. It was the oldest and wisest man of the village, who scolded them sharply.

"Silly children, all of you!" he thundered. "If you go in anger, if you go without a plan, then I can promise that you never will return. You'll be crushed beneath the rocks, just like the villagers in Wayfarer's story."

And hearing him, the people dropped their weapons, ashamed to think what they had almost done.

"Grandfather, help us," they begged.

"Yes," he replied, "if you give me the time to consult with the spirits."

And he closed himself inside his lodge for several days, and there he asked for wisdom, and there he made a plan. Calling Wayfarer, he whispered, "Tell me what you think of this." And Wayfarer listened as the old man explained what he thought it best to do.

"Yes," said the Wayfarer. "I think that it will work." Then Wayfarer took a spear, went toward the cave of the Bush-Tailed Rat Man, and hid himself among the rocks.

Meanwhile, the old man called the villagers to gather round and said to them, "Now is the time for us to visit the Bush-Tailed Rat Man." And he led them to the cave.

The Bush-Tailed Rat Man saw them coming and opened his door as he had to the people of Wayfarer's village.

"Come in, come in, my friends," he called as they approached.

The old man answered, "Yes, of course. But first come down and tell me if you recognize this flower growing here beside the path. I've never seen anything like it before."

Leaving the door to his cave standing open, the Bush-Tailed Rat Man came down to look at the flower. It was just a common violet, he explained, saying, "Surely your eyes have grown dim with age, or else you would have known the flower's name."

"A violet? Certainly not," replied the old man. "Look, don't you see this orange streak?" And with questions like this, he kept the Bush-Tailed Rat Man occupied, while Wayfarer crept from the rocks where he was hidden and placed a spear across the top of the entrance to the cave, where no one could see it, so that the door could not be closed.

That done, Wayfarer limped to the side of the Rat Man and said, "Oh, grandfather, I fear your sight is failing. This flower is a violet, just as the Rat Man has told you."

"Ah, well," said the old man, "perhaps you are right." Then he said to the Rat Man, "May we enter your lodging?"

"Come right in," said the Rat Man. And he entered his cave with all the other people, never guessing at the danger he was in. Once inside, the people circled him and shouted, "Now we have you where we want you! Show us where to find our missing children and our food."

"How should I know where they are?" exclaimed the Bush-Tailed Rat Man, thinking very fast. "If you suppose that I have stolen them, you're wrong, absolutely wrong. I swear to you, I have no idea where they could be. But let me try to help. Surely, you are hungry. Wait here, and I shall fetch you food from cellars I have dug outside."

"Don't take a step," the people shouted; "we're not so stupid as you think!"

But suddenly, and much to their amazement, the old man said, "Silly children, let him go. Can't you see he wants to help you?" And making a path through the crowd of angry villagers, he walked with the Rat Man to the door of the cave.

In a flash, the Rat Man leapt outside and, hoping to trap the villagers, cried to the door, "Snap shut!" But because of Wayfarer's spear, the door wouldn't budge—not even an inch. The Bush-Tailed Rat Man cried, "Snap shut," until his voice grew hoarse, and still the door stayed open.

Now, seeing that he'd been outfoxed, the Rat Man turned to run away. But he did not run for long or travel far. As he stumbled down the path, the clever old man called out a curse, and the Bush-Tailed Rat Man changed from a man into a rat, just a common bush-tailed rat, who forever after was no bigger than a pine cone and squeaked as he ran among the rocks.

The people all rejoiced to see his sorry end. And they cheered when the old man called after him, "For your evil ways, you will never be a man again, but always a bush-tailed rat. Your food will be the garbage that you find in cold damp cellars, and your home will be a hole between the rocks. Go, and be sorry for the sadness that you've caused."

Then, turning to the villagers, the old man said, "Now you see what a plan can accomplish! The Rat Man has become a rat, and you're alive instead of dead, and the door to the cave will stand open while you look for what you've lost."

"Yes," the people said, and thanked him warmly, for without him they would certainly have failed.

Now they searched the cave and found its hidden cellars—found their stolen food and missing children. And they cried with tears of happiness to gaze upon those lovely fresh young faces, which they'd never thought to see again. Gratefully, they all embraced the children, and also hugged each other, and most of all praised Wayfarer, whose tale had made this happy moment possible.

"Oh, Wayfarer," they told him, "you've given us our children back again. Come stay with us and we will make you happy for as long as you shall live."

"Too kind, you are too kind," said Wayfarer modestly. "I haven't done as much as you suppose. And in any case, I think I'm born to travel, as my name suggests. But if you'll give me your permission, I'll gladly return to your village for friendship and rest as I wander here and there throughout the forest."

"You shall always be welcome," said the people.

And thanking them, Wayfarer set out again on his journey. Swish went his poor, lame foot through the leaves. Crackle went the forest twigs that snapped beneath his other foot, the good one. And loudly he sang his brave new song:

Bush-Tailed Rat, the man you used to be
Is now an ugly rodent,
Squeaking pitifully.
Stealing bits of rubbish, that's all that you can do;
Bush-Tailed Rat, we're
Rid of you!

Why the Indians Changed Their Home

My name, the name my parents gave me, is Born-to-Swim-Alone. The story I tell happened a long time ago, a time when I was but a child, a time in which the white face came. In those days, the place where we had made our home was fresh and green, and fishes, numerous as stones, filled the rushing stream.

Our tribe lived along a large lake, with the forest as our neighbor. Streams fed the lake waters, which were close by the sea. As children, my friends and I dug clams on the beach called Waves-Striking-Forehead. Our fathers fished for herring and for crabs, both large and small. They speared river trout and in wooden traps caught silver salmon, which they cut in half, roasted, and placed on drying poles, for all to share.

The forest behind our village teemed with creatures famous for their skins: bears, brown and black; elk, fat, with large antlers; and woolly mountain goats. Deer ran everywhere. The forest smelled of pine needles and of bushes heavily hung with red berries and blue. Rabbits and squirrels and foxes scampered across the pine-needle floor of the forest, a floor so soft and quiet our hunters never could be heard as they crept through the woods in search of deer meat for our feasts.

In spring, the wind brought us birds, with brightly colored feathers, and the air rang with birdsong. We collected gull eggs in the rocks and duck eggs from their nests. Our fathers caught geese and other birds of the air. They harpooned seals and dug up clover roots, which the children steamed on red hot stones.

No one was hungry. Our people were well fed and warm.

Dressed skin was plentiful and nearly everyone wore animal furs. Our fishing and hunting grounds were always full, because we hunted not for sport, but just for food and clothes. Sickness was a stranger. Our days were rich with laughter.

Then the white face came, came when we were sleeping, came to spoil, not to share. He came looking for animal skins, skins to sell, not to keep the cold from his bones. He came out of the forest one night and asked our chief, whose name was Oldest-One-in-the-World, for a place to rest. It was the winter. It was dark. Snow covered the ground. Oldest-One-in-the-World invited the white face into his house. He called the white face guest, gave him the best seat, sat him by the fire, gave him furs to warm him, fed him elk meat, and said the white face would be treated like one of his own children.

The white face asked Oldest-One-in-the-World where the canoes were kept, and the skins, and the dried meat, and the berries. Oldest-One-in-the-World told him that the canoes were at the forest edge and showed him where our storage houses stood. The white face asked whether the house of Oldest-One-in-the-World was the house of the chief. Oldest-One-in-the-World did not know why the white face asked him all these questions, but still he spoke the truth.

"The house you are in is the home of the chief," he said. "This house is the center of the village. The best place in my house is next to the fire, where you are sitting. The doors of my house look out upon the forest and the lake, from which places we gather our food."

When the white face left our village, he placed a necklace of beads around the neck of Oldest-One-in-the-World and said that he would never hunt our meat, nor fish our salmon pools. But he did not keep his word. When spring came, the white face came again, came with many men who carried magic poles, poles that shot not wooden arrows but balls of fire.

One night when we were sitting on the beach, listening to Moon-in-Sky's story about how Little Twig urged his brother branches to stick together so they could not be snapped by the wind, the white faces stole through the forest to the place where our canoes were kept and set fire to them. Then they broke into our storehouse and took our food and furs. When we ran to get bows and arrows, they surrounded the house of Oldest-One-in-the-World, who had hurt his foot and could not join us on the beach.

"If you come any closer," yelled one of the white faces, "we will burn the house of your chief—with him in it."

Seeing there was nothing to be done, our people put down their pointed arrows and their bows and let the white faces escape into the forest, carrying with them our furs and food.

A few days later, the white faces returned shooting fire through their magic poles. Many of our people died. But we managed with our arrows to drive the white faces off, off into the forest, which now to us was out of bounds because the white faces camped there. Hereafter, we could feed ourselves only by fishing for salmon. But soon the white faces rolled large stones into the river and formed a wall, so the salmon couldn't reach our traps.

Then a message came, a message from the white faces. You must burn your bows and arrows, it said. Your land and work will now belong to us. Agree or die.

Oldest-One-in-the-World called our people together and explained that we would have to fight or run away. If we fought, we'd all be killed by the magic poles of fire. But if we ran away, the forest would not be our friend, for that was where the white faces hid. And the lake that lay before us like a vast unbroken meadow, the lake that we had skimmed across

so many times before, had now become a dark and frightening hole in which, without our strong canoes, we'd disappear. Escape across the lake was possible, he said, only for those who could swim a long distance, but not for the weak, the old, or the newborn, who, he reminded us, could not be left behind or be allowed to drown. Help must be found.

"We require," said Oldest-One-in-the-World, "a magical medicine man, a shaman, who can summon up the spirits of the earth—the spirits we call Manitous—and put them to work for us."

"A shaman," cried a young man, "who will burn the forest and drive away the white faces."

Oldest-One-in-the-World shook his head and explained that we needed Manitous who'd help us, but who would do the earth no harm. For if we harmed the earth, we harmed ourselves. The earth, said Oldest-One-in-the-World, is a woman and the mother of all people. She has flesh, which is the soil. The trees and flowers and grasses are her hair, and the rocks her bones. The wind is her breath, the rain her tears. She shivers when cold. She sweats when hot. Every time she moves, we have an earthquake. But some people, he said, have forgotten who their mother is and have treated the earth badly, burning and scarring her skin, gouging her body and tearing her hair. She is still alive, but will not help us if we hurt her. This land, he said, this land the white face wants, this village, is part of our mother's body, which she gave us to live and rest upon. We know whence we came. We know our ancestors. We have inhabited this country for a long time. The earth is full of the bones of our ancestors. We shall not hurt the earth.

"Born-to-Swim-Alone," he called, "come here."

The blood rushed to my head. My body trembled. What could Oldest-One-in-the-World want of me, a boy who'd only seen the spring a dozen times?

"Born-to-Swim-Alone, you are young and strong," said Oldest-One-in-the-World. "You swim like the silver salmon, upstream and down. Tonight when the moon has slid behind the clouds and the white faces cannot see you, you will swim across the lake to the land beyond the water. There you will find many Indian villages, and in each village a shaman. Ask each one if his great magic can help us. Tell them that we are in prison, surrounded, and that our lands and food and furs have been spoiled or stolen from us. Tell them that the white face

wants to destroy us, that we have very little time to live. Tell them that we must find a way to escape to a new land, where we may multiply and be happy."

"How will I carry the shamans back across the lake?" I asked.

"They will have to swim," said Oldest-One-in-the-World, "because if the white faces see them coming by canoe, they'll kill them."

That night I set out. The evening lake was cold. The stones at the water's edge were dark and slick with moss. I feared that I would slip and make a splashing noise. To keep from being heard, I sat down in the water, slid on my stomach, and slowly drifted toward the deep. When I was far enough from shore, I started to swim, slowly at first, in keeping with the rhythm of the lapping water, and then more quickly. I remembered to stroke evenly and breathe deeply, as I was taught by Wind-on-Water, who taught me how to swim when I was just a child. Although I had never tried before to cross the lake, I had gone to the middle, so I knew that the distance was not too great for me to cover. In an hour I reached the distant shore, where several Indians from the Lytton tribe helped me up the beach and covered me with blankets. I was taken to their village, where I was given something hot to drink and met their chief, to whom I told my story.

"You will not have to go from tribe to tribe," he said. "You have come far enough for one so young. I will send messengers to all the neighboring tribes, and also to those along the coast. They will return with the most powerful shamans, those who can make the clouds gather and the sky roar. In the meantime, you will be my guest."

I was then taken to the chief's house, where I was given food and a warm place to sleep. That night the messengers set out, running down the forest paths and along the sandy coast. So quickly did they run that by mid-afternoon of the next day, five shamans, two who came by horse and three by foot, had reached the Lytton village, ready to cross the lake that very evening. Each of the shamans had great power—one over the fog, one over the wind, one over the rain, one over the heat, and one over the cold. When they asked how they were to reach my village, I told them we would have to swim. But Cloud-on-Ground, the shaman who had power over the fog, said that he had never learned, so I agreed to take him on my back. That night, the six of us entered the water.

At first, Cloud-on-Ground wrapped his arms around my neck; and as I swam, he rested on my back. But before we'd reached the middle of the lake, his weight began to tire me; so I told him to roll over on his back and I would put my hand beneath his chin and pull him as I swam. At first the thought of floating on his back frightened him. He stiffened his arms and legs; I thought he'd drag me under. But when the shaman Sun-in-Sky told him to rest as lightly on the water as a leaf, he grew calm and let his muscles loosen up. Then I shifted to my side, swimming with one arm, and using the other to tow him along. When at last we reached the other side, Oldest-One-in-the-World said a prayer thanking the lake spirits for carrying us safely to him.

We were taken to the council fire and there we sat, eating bear meat to make us strong, while Oldest-One-in-the-World praised me for my courage and thanked the shamans for their willingness to help.

"When the mountain sheep is chased by the wolf," said Oldest-One-in-the-World, "the sheep must either trick the wolf or kill himself, because he will not let the wolf devour him. We, as well, must either trick the white faces—and by this means escape—or kill ourselves. For we will not be devoured by the white faces."

Oldest-One-in-the-World then commanded that more logs be added to the fire and that the dances should begin. The fire leapt and the logs groaned, as sparks flashed in the evening air. The dancers formed a circle and, shaking their beaded arms and legs, swept round and round until the fire reached high enough to warm the lower reaches of the sky. The rhythmic clapping of hands, and stamping of feet, caused us all, young and old, to sway from side to side in time with the music.

The shamans whom I'd led across the lake sat upon the ground, rocking back and forth, softly chanting. With their eyes closed and their arms extended toward the fire, they began to chant louder and louder, their voices rising to a fevered pitch. All the while the fire raged, and the dancers whirled faster and faster, their bodies glistening with sweat In the light of the logs, as the shamans uttered sounds like none that I had ever heard before. In the midst of the ceremony, Oldest-One-in-the-World slowly rose from the place of honor. He stood absolutely still. Then he held up one hand to signal for silence.

"The time has come," he said, "for our great shamans to present us with their magic, and to show us how we might escape our enemies."

For a minute no one moved. The only sounds came from the burning logs and the lake, where the water softly splashed around the stones. The air was still; tree leaves glistened in the moonlight. It was hard to believe that just a short distance away, in the forest, the white faces camped.

"Cloud-on-Ground," called Oldest-One-in-the-World. "You have power over the fog. Show us how you will save us from our enemies. Show us how you will lead us from this land to safety."

Cloud-on-Ground stood up, walked once around the council fire, then reached into the flames and quickly pulled a sapling from among the burning logs. Without a word, he put the smoking piece of wood upon the ground some distance from the council fire. Out of a leather pouch, he took some elk hair and a beaver's toe, which he threw on the smoldering sapling. Then he uttered a loud cry, put a pine cone on the fire, and with his hand drew a circle round his head. Suddenly the air grew moist and heavy. The earth beneath our feet began to ooze a heavy sweat.

"Fog of the earth, fog of the sky," chanted Cloud-on-Ground, "blanket forest, ferns, and firefly."

The entire village was immediately engulfed by fog. Fog on the lake, fog in the forest. Fog up the coast, fog down the coast. Fog everywhere. A thick wet blanket hung across the land. Our council fire disappeared. I could not see the person sitting next to me. I stood up. With arms and hands outstretched, I found myself groping through the mist to feel my way. Then, fearing I would walk into the lake, I got down on my hands and knees and crawled along the ground. But after a while I even had to give up crawling,

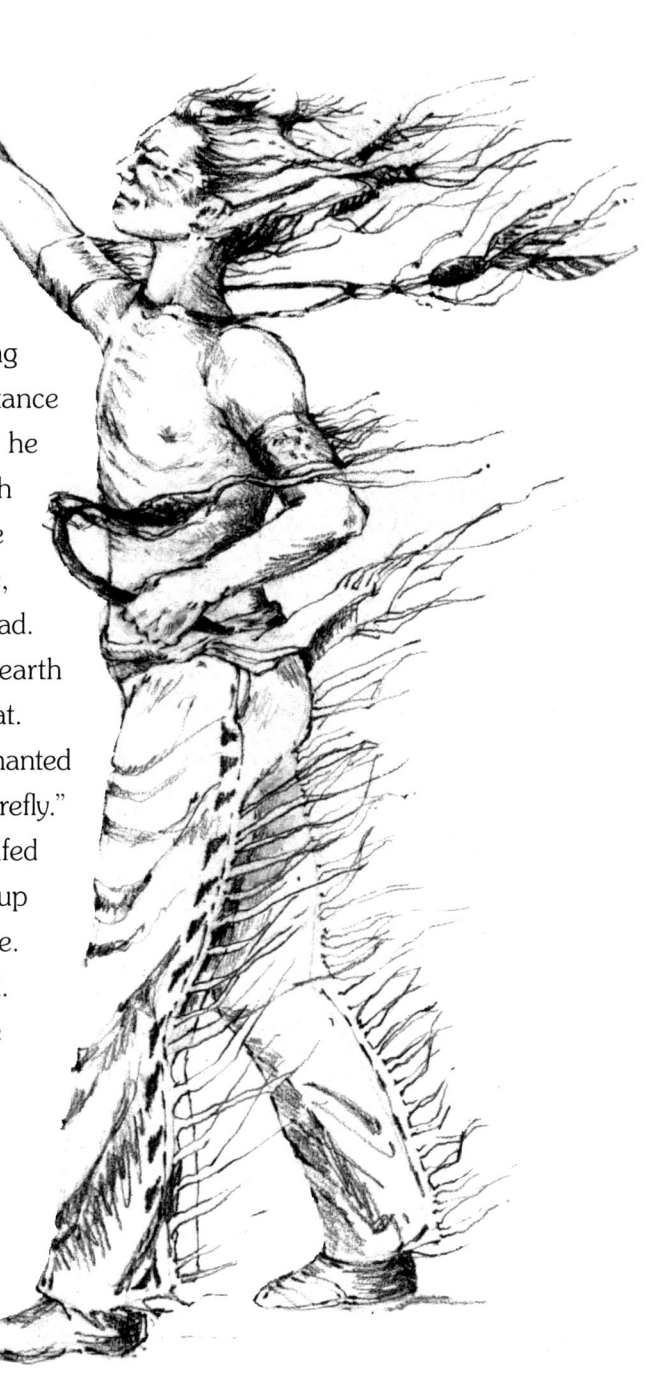

because I could not see to move.

"Enough," called Oldest-One-in-the-World, whose voice came sharply through the fog. "If we cannot see, we cannot run away. Cloud-on-Ground, call back the fog. Put it away. For our people to escape, we'll need a different kind of magic."

In an instant, the fog vanished and the council fire returned. Cloud-on-Ground, still standing by the smoldering sapling, tucked away in his leather pouch the last of the fog and said how sad he was his magic couldn't help us.

"You are a good man," said Oldest-One-in-the-World. "You tried to find a way for us to cross the lake. We won't forget your kindness."

"It is my turn," said Wind-in-Mountains, rising from the council fire. With this remark, he poked the vacant air, danced a slow majestic dance, and then repeated three times the magic words: *wa lae em lae ba*. Suddenly from the mountain tops a great wind roared down across the forest, the village, and the lake. The air was filled with leaves and limbs torn from trees, and with cooking pots and blankets from the village. Great waves formed on the lake. The council fire blew out. Ash and sparks flew everywhere. We could neither sit nor stand. The wind tossed us about like desert tumbleweed. One gust flung me near a cedar tree, which I grabbed and held as tightly as I could, hoping that we wouldn't be uprooted in the wind.

"Enough," shouted Oldest-One-in-the-World, whose voice in the howling wind could hardly be heard. "If we are unable to sit or stand and if the world is falling down around us, we cannot run away. Wind-in-Mountains, call back the wind. Put it away. For our people to escape, we'll need a different kind of magic."

In a second, the wind stopped and the council fire flared up again. But Wind-in-Mountains had not resumed his seat. He stood with both hands clenched.

"It will take a few minutes," he said, "for the wind, which I am holding tightly in my hands, to die down. Then I'll be able to open my fists."

Before long, he slowly relaxed his grip and opened his hands. Not a whisper of wind could be heard in the air. All was now still.

"You are a good man," said Oldest-One-in-the-World. "You tried to find a way for us to cross the lake. We won't forget your kindness."

"Let me be next," said Rain-off-Raven's-Back. I think that I can help."

Oldest-One-in-the-World agreed. Then Rain-off-Raven's-Back reached into a furry bag he had tied around his waist and removed a grizzly bear mask. Putting on the mask, he danced around the fire seven times, each time singing a different song. All at once, the skies

turned dark with black clouds overhead. Thunder rolled above us. The council fire died. The air grew damp and cool. Then it began to rain, and rain, and rain, the water coming down as thick as blankets. In no time, large puddles formed; a minute later, the water was up to our ankles and the ground beneath our feet grew swampy. Then the lake began to rise, and the waters crept closer to our village.

"The rain," said Rain-off-Raven's-Back, "will drive the white face from the forest and then you, Oldest-One-in-the-World, and your people, will be safe."

Oldest-One-in-the-World, whose wet clothes hung on him like skins on drying racks, replied, "The water will not drown our enemies. It will flood our village. You must call back the rain."

Putting on his mask again, Rain-off-Raven's-Back danced around the fire in the opposite direction, and just as quickly as the rain had come it vanished clean away. The lake receded, the council fire burst into flame, and the ground grew dry beneath our feet.

"You are a good man," said Oldest-One-in-the-World. "You tried to find a way for us to cross the lake. We won't forget your kindness."

Sun-in-Sky, a shaman known far and wide along the coast, then rose from the council fire and said to Oldest-One-in-the-World, "My powers are so great that I'm afraid to use them. Maybe it would be better for your people if they went into the sweat-houses to purify themselves and prayed to the great spirits for help."

"We have prayed for a shaman like yourself," said Oldest-One-in-the-World, "to show us how to free ourselves, since we are trapped between the forest and the lake. In the forest are the white faces, who've burned all of our canoes. In the lake is water so deep that many of our people cannot cross it. We rely on you to find a way across the lake."

"All right, then," said Sun-in-Sky, "I will use a powerful manitou to dry up all the water, which will allow you to escape across the lake bed." Calling for Fox, he shouted, "Fox, come forth from the forest. Fox, come out of the woods." In an instant, Fox came running through the trees along the lake, stopping at our council fire. "Run to the top of the mountain," said Sun-in-Sky, "and tell Brother Sun to come close and shine bright on this village and this lake, so close and bright that the land will be parched and the lake will dry up." Fox turned and ran back along the beach and then darted for the forest.

Before I had time to stir the embers of the council fire, the sun grew bright in the sky and the embers burned up in a flash. As the temperature rose, the flowers wilted, the grass died, and the trees lost their leaves. And still the temperature rose. We jumped into the lake to cool off; but the water grew hotter and hotter, until it began to steam. Then we ran back to our houses to escape the blistering sun. And still the temperature rose. The lake waters began to dry up, and trees caught fire, and our houses began to smoke.

"We will perish from the heat," cried Oldest-One-in-the-World. "Before the lake dries up, we'll be destroyed. And even if the lake should dry up first, the ground will be too hot to step on. The earth will be like fire. Call back the heat, Sun-in-Sky. Put away the sun."

"I warned you," said Sun-in-Sky, "to be wary of my magic. It is too strong to be loosed upon the earth."

Then once again, Sun-in-Sky called forth Fox from the forest.

"Go," he said, "to the top of the mountain and tell Brother Sun to return to the place in the sky from which he came."

Immediately, Fox took off for the mountain. No sooner was he gone than the sun turned round in the sky and the earth began to cool. The waters of the lake returned, the flowers bloomed, the grass greened, and the trees leafed.

"You are a good man," said Oldest-One-in-the-World. "You tried to find a way for us to cross the lake. We won't forget your kindness."

All eyes then turned to Moon-in-Snow.

"I am a member of the Salishan tribe," he said, "unfamiliar with the ways of water. My magic is for curing ills, not escaping enemies. But I will summon moon and cold to see if they can help you."

He then retired to one of the lodges, where he prepared his magic. When he returned, his hair, which had been tied together with hemlock twigs, hung loose around his shoulders. His face was colored red with ocher, his body yellow with pollen from the fir tree. He wore a necklace of abalone shells and his arms rattled with copper bracelets. Around his elbows, knees, and ankles he had wrapped leather straps, and around his middle he wore a woolen belt. Wrapping himself in a blanket made from the skins of sea otter, he held up his hand to indicate he wished to speak.

"The skin of otter," he said, "will guide me in matters bearing on the water."

It was now late at night. Moon-in-Snow took a pointed stick and made a circle in the sand, where moonlight struck the beach. He asked for the tail feathers of an eagle and when they were given to him, he waved them three times over the circle, chanting the name *Quo-Mogwa*. Then he jumped over the circle four times. As his feet touched the sand on the last jump, a cold wind began to blow. The council fire failed. The temperature dropped. One minute a chill was in the air, the next a frost. The ground grew cold and hard. Tree leaves began to glisten with the frost. Branches stiffened. And still the temperature dropped. We fled to our lodges, covered ourselves with bear blankets, and lit log fires to keep warm. Still the temperature dropped. Snow fell, collecting in the village. The wind howled. We huddled in our lodges, so cold we couldn't sleep.

Oldest-One-in-the-World called Moon-in-Snow to his lodge, telling him that he must call back the cold before the people froze to death. But he refused, saying they must be patient if his magic was to work. The next morning, when we looked out of our lodges, the sight that met our eyes was magical. Thick ice covered the lake. We had never before seen the lake turned to ice. We gathered up our belongings and assembled on the beach, where Moon-in-Snow told us to move across the lake as quickly as we could, for the white faces would soon be coming after us.

Sure enough, as we were crossing the lake, the white faces came running from the forest. But we had started early in the morning and had gone too far for them to catch us. When we had reached the distant shore, the white faces, in the middle of the frozen lake, still were coming after us. Moon-in-Snow looked round and asked if all of us had safely crossed. When we assured him that we had, he snapped his fingers in the air and the lake that had a moment earlier been frozen thick with winter ice now turned to summer water. With a snap of his fingers, the white face disappeared—and my people settled elsewhere.

I am now an aged man, a skin upon a stick. But the story I have told is one that all my people sing about until their dying day.

The Story of Hot and Cold

Heat-Man's parents died when he was just a baby. They had traveled to the cold country and had been overcome by snow and ice. So Heat-Man's grandmother raised him and also his brothers. He learned many things from her, like how to tell the hour of the day from the position of the sun, how to make the warm winds blow, and how to find the richest salmon pools; but she never taught him how to find a wife.

He was now a young man and wanted to marry. But there were no young women in his village. Not knowing what to do, he took to his bed and lay there sick at heart. His grandmother asked what ailed him, but he was at a loss for words. He was embarrassed to tell her, so he said nothing. She questioned him many times, but he would not reply. Then one day, his grandmother, remembering how silent she had been when she had wanted to get married, guessed his secret.

"You want a wife," she said. "I can tell that you are lonely." Heat-Man nodded and said yes. When his elder brothers came home, she asked them if they knew a village where

Heat-Man could find a wife. They said the finest girls that they had heard about lived at the other end of the earth, in the cold country. Their names were Ice-Flower and Snow-Bird, and they were the daughters of Cold. Though the brothers had neither met nor seen these sisters, they'd been told that they were just alike in everything but magic, where Snow-Bird was the more gifted of the two.

"You must not go there," said his grandmother. "No one can travel to the cold country and return alive. Your parents went there and died."

But Heat-Man wanted to go. He wanted to succeed where his parents had failed. Convinced that he could overcome the ice and snow, he insisted on journeying to this frigid place and marrying Snow-Bird, the younger daughter of Cold. His grandmother, who feared for his life, tried to change his mind.

"Don't go," she pleaded. "Choose a wife from among our relatives, from among our cousins who live near the middle of the earth."

But Heat-Man would not change his mind. He kept repeating that he would go to the cold country and marry Snow-Bird, the younger daughter of Cold. His grandmother had no choice except to teach him what she knew about the secrets of the ice and of the people who had built their houses on it.

"When you reach the cold country," she said, "if you are not to freeze, you must wear the fur of bear, and if you are not to die in Snow-Bird's house, you must know what to answer when she asks you to sit on a chair of ice."

Then she went to her bed and removed from underneath the pillow a golden staff, an eight-inch stick that looked exactly like a magic wand.

"Take it," she said, giving Heat-Man the staff. "It will save you from the ice chair, but not from any other tests."

Heat-Man looked surprised. He hadn't known that to win the hand of Snow-Bird, there'd be a test he'd have to pass. His grandmother explained to him that beauty is not won without an effort.

"When Snow-Bird invites you to sit on the ice chair," said the grandmother, "you must put the golden staff on the chair before you sit. Otherwise, you'll stick to the seat and freeze to death. The golden staff will keep you warm and protect you from the chair."

Heat-Man took the golden staff and thanked his grandmother for her help. "But is this," he asked, "the only test I'll have to overcome?"

"No," she said. "You'll have to pass three others that Snow-Bird's father, Cold, will put you through. And if you pass those tests, you may have to face some other ones as well. But I am old and cannot read the future as clearly now as I did once before."

"Try, grandmother," said Heat-Man, "try to see the days ahead. Tell me what will happen, and how should I proceed?"

His grandmother thought for a long time. She was looking through the present to the future. Finally, she shook her head and smiled. She had seen the outline of something else to come.

"Snow-Bird will offer you advice on how to pass the tests, and you must do exactly as she says," said his grandmother. "Unless you follow her instructions, you will die."

Then she snapped her fingers and down from the top of the mountain flew an eagle, the grandmother's servant.

"Deliver my grandson safely to the cold country," she said.

Heat-Man took the golden staff and put it in his shirt. Then he climbed up on the eagle. In a minute they were flying high above the clouds.

When they had passed over the middle of the earth, the eagle directed Heat-Man to look off to the north.

"You see in the distance those four snowy mountaintops?" asked the eagle. "We must fly beyond the farthest one to get to the cold country, where Cold lives with his wife and two daughters. They live in three houses. Cold and his wife live in the first house, Ice-Flower lives in the second, and Snow-Bird in the third."

After what seemed like hours in the sky, the eagle began to float toward earth, slowly downward, downward slowly, until it hovered over the houses of the Cold family. Gliding toward the house of the younger daughter, the eagle lightly landed at the front door. Heat-Man slid to the ground, thanked the eagle for bringing him to the other end of the world, and sent it back to his grandmother in the heat country.

Going up to Snow-Bird's door, Heat-Man knocked and entered. When she asked him who he was and why he'd come, he told her of his loneliness.

"I no longer want to be alone," he said. "I want you for my wife. I have come all the way from the heat country to marry you."

Snow-Bird said that she was flattered and invited him to sit upon a chair she'd made of ice. He quickly took his golden staff from underneath his shirt and, when Snow-Bird looked away, he laid the staff across the chair and sat upon the staff.

"Is the chair comfortable?" she asked, fully expecting him to stick to the ice chair and freeze to death.

"Very comfortable," he answered. "I like the coolness of the chair. It's quite relaxing."

Snow-Bird thought that Heat-Man was trying to trick her. So she asked him to stand up. She was sure that he'd be caught, stuck to the ice chair.

"Look at the bird on the windowsill," he said, in order to distract her.

Then he leapt up and put the staff back in his shirt. When she looked at him again, he was standing and the chair had turned to gold.

"I must choose you for my husband," said Snow-Bird. "No one else has ever freed himself from the ice chair. But my father will test you, and you must do exactly as I tell you. If you follow my instructions, all will be well. If not, you will die."

Heat-Man agreed to do everything that he was told. He knew from his grandmother's warning that Snow-Bird's instructions would save his life. She then told him about the three tests that her father would make him pass.

"The first test," she said, "involves the mountain you see in the distance, the one covered all with ice. On the other side is a spring of water. My father will ask you to take that spring of water and place it in front of his house, where it will have to run without freezing."

Heat-Man wasn't sure that he could pass the test.

"You must," she said, "because the second test is even harder than the first. My father will ask you to make a large lake near his house and then to gather up all the ducks in the cold country and put them on the lake."

"I'm afraid that I will fail," said Heat-Man. "To round up all the ducks could take a dozen years or more."

"To make the second test more difficult," explained Snow-Bird, "my father will make an icy wind blow across the lake, and you must keep the lake from freezing. Otherwise, the ducks will fly away."

Shaking his head and groaning, Heat-Man said that it would take the power of the sun to keep the waters of the lake from turning into ice.

"The third test is the worst," said Snow-Bird. "It will require you to make a large corral with walls of stone. And into this corral, you must drive all the forest animals: the bears, caribou, deer, elk, foxes, porcupines, raccoons, squirrels, wolverines, and others."

Holding his head, Heat-Man began to sigh. He knew that to gather up all the ducks in the cold country was just about impossible; but to round up all the forest animals could surely not be done.

"How am I to do it?" he asked Snow-Bird.

"I will tell you how," she said. "I will give you magic. During these tests, you must think of nothing else but me. If your mind wanders, you will die. When you think of me, I shall be there to help you; but you'll not see me, because I'll be invisible. Now go to my father's house."

Heat-Man went to Cold's house and knocked at the door. Cold told his wife to open it. He asked Heat-Man what he wanted.

"I want to marry Snow-Bird."

"Very well," said Cold. "If you pass the three tests I shall give you, you may marry my daughter. But first you must make me a promise."

"Anything," said Heat-Man.

"You must promise me that if you pass the tests and marry Snow-Bird, you will live with our people and never leave the country of the cold."

"I promise," said Heat-Man.

Then Cold warned him that if he didn't pass all three tests, he would die. He warned him, too, that he would die if he married Snow-Bird and ever tried to leave the country of the cold.

Heat-Man agreed to all the terms and said that he was anxious to begin the tests.

"The first test," said Cold, "is to bring to my front door the spring of water that lies on the other side of the ice mountain. But you mustn't let the water freeze."

Heat-Man, thinking of Snow-Bird and nothing else, hiked up and over the mountain of ice until he came to the spring of water. Then he drew a line along the ground from the spring all the way back to Cold's house. Silently, Heat-Man prayed that Snow-Bird would turn the line in the dirt into a ditch, a ditch that would carry the spring water from the mountain to Cold's front door. And sure enough, when Heat-Man looked over his shoulder, he saw the water following close behind him running through the ditch. In the morning, Cold opened his front door and there in front of him was a small creek gurgling past his house.

Puffing himself up, Cold blew a freezing wind across the creek to turn it into ice, but Heat-Man knew what he must do. Puffing himself up, Heat-Man blew a hot wind into the cold wind. As a result, the creek didn't freeze.

"You surprise me," said Cold; "but there is more that you must do. The second test is to create a lake just a short distance from my house. And on that lake I want to see all the ducks in the cold country."

That night, Heat-Man found a good place for a lake close to Cold's house. Making a mark upon the ground and thinking of Snow-Bird and nothing else, Heat-Man spread his arms and made the sign of a lake. Suddenly a large lake appeared. Then he moved his arms in a wide circle, as if gathering to him something in the air. Immediately, great numbers of ducks appeared in the sky; in a minute they flew down and settled on the waters of the lake.

The next morning, Cold saw the lake and, puffing himself up, blew a freezing wind across the water to drive the ducks away; but Heat-Man knew what he must do. Putting his golden staff in the lake, he stirred the water all about, so the temperature was not too cold and not too hot, but just right for the ducks. As a result, they didn't fly away.

"I see you have great magic of your own," said Cold; "but there is more that you must do. The third test is to make a large corral surrounded by a wall of stone. Into this corral, you're to drive all the forest animals, from the smallest to the largest, from the chipmunk to the bear."

Again, Heat-Man started out at night. Thinking of Snow-Bird and nothing else, he wished a thousand stones would thunder down the mountainside and fall in perfect order. No sooner had he thought this thought than a large corral appeared—and all the forest animals came running, one after another, right into the pen.

In the morning, Cold saw the corral with all the forest animals penned within the walls. He was very angry because he did not want to lose his daughter. So he said that before Heat-Man could marry Snow-Bird, he would have to pass one last test.

Snow-Bird, taking Heat-Man aside, whispered in his ear, "My father will put my sister and me in a room. Then, because we look so much alike, he will ask you which of us you want to be your wife. Our dress and hair will be the same, so you won't be able to tell us apart. If you choose my sister, my father will say you do not love me and will kill you. You must therefore pick Snow-Bird and not Ice-Flower."

"But how will I know?" whispered Heat-Man.

"Look into our eyes," answered Snow-Bird. "When you look at me, I shall wink; then you'll know which of us to pick."

Just as Snow-Bird predicted, her father placed the sisters in a room. Ice-Flower and Snow-Bird were dressed exactly alike and had fixed their hair the same way. When Heat-Man entered the room, he couldn't tell them apart. Cold was watching his daughters closely. Heat-Man began to worry. How could Snow-Bird wink, with her father looking at her? What if Snow-Bird failed to remember to wink? What if both sisters winked? He walked up to one sister. She smiled at him. He walked up to the other sister. She also smiled at him. No one winked.

"Well, which one is Snow-Bird?" asked Cold. "Make your choice."

"I will have to look more closely," answered Heat-Man.

This time he put his face so close to the first sister that they were nearly rubbing noses. By standing this close, Heat-Man knew that Cold would have no way of seeing if his daughter winked. The first sister only smiled. He put his face close to the second sister. She smiled—and then suddenly winked.

"This," said Heat-Man, "is Snow-Bird. It is she I want for my wife."

Cold was very disappointed. He did not want to lose his daughter. But he knew it wasn't fair to make Heat-Man undergo another test.

"You have performed all the tasks," said Cold. "I therefore accept you as my son-in-law. You may marry Snow-Bird and live with her in her house. But you must never attempt to take her away from the cold country. You must live with us always."

Heat-Man thanked Cold for letting him marry Snow-Bird and promised not to leave. But Cold wanted to be sure that Heat-Man kept his promise, so he put in Snow-Bird's house a magic flute. Whenever the couple left the house, the flute played music loudly. Thus Cold knew when the couple were and were not home.

For four years, Heat-Man and Snow-Bird lived in the cold country. They now had a son, three years old, called Morning-Light, who chattered like a magpie. Often he would ask why he never got to feel the heat of the sun.

"Why don't we ever visit the heat country?" he would say to his father. I want to play outside in the warm air that you so often talk about."

Heat-Man explained that he'd promised never to leave the country of the cold. Morning-Light cried. He cried that he wanted to feel the heat of the sun. One day, Morning-Light began to cough. Snow-Bird could not stand to see him sick, so she asked her husband why they couldn't travel to his country, where the sun could cure their Morning-Light.

"You know the reason," said Heat-Man. "I promised your father we would never leave."

Snow-Bird did not want to disobey her father's wishes, but Morning-Light's coughing was more than she could bear.

"Let us go to the heat country. Our son coughs all the time and the sun will do him good."

Heat-Man was afraid that Cold would kill them if they tried to leave. He also feared that Morning-Light would die from his cough if they stayed. Snow-Bird, too, was fearful for the child. She pleaded with Heat-Man, saying that she knew how to trick her father and escape. At last, Heat-Man gave in. He agreed to take Snow-Bird and Morning-Light to his country.

That night, when all was dark, they packed up their belongings and prepared to travel south. He told the flute not to play after they had left the house. Then they crept into the night. But the flute belonged to Cold and was faithful to his wishes. So shortly after Heat-Man and his family had run off, the flute began to play. Cold, hearing the music, sent his wife to find out why the flute was playing in the middle of the night. She came back a minute later, out of breath, to report that the young people were gone.

"Go after them immediately," ordered Cold. "Bring them back to me; for if I go myself, I fear that I will lose my temper and freeze them all to death."

Off she ran, quick as the wind. But Snow-Bird saw her mother coming in the distance.

"My mother is chasing us," said Snow-Bird, "and will catch us before we get away. To save us, I shall use the magic that my father taught me."

Saying the magic words *kaylogwis kwek waxa we*, Snow-Bird, as fast as light, turned Heat-Man into an old duck, Morning-Light into a duckling, and herself into a lake. When her mother arrived, she saw nothing but a small lake with two ducks on it. The young people were nowhere to be found, so she returned and told her husband what she'd seen.

"Those were our children," said Cold to his wife. "Our daughter is strong in magic and has tricked you. She has used magic that I taught her. Go after them again. But this time, do not let her trick you."

Cold's wife set out again. And again, Snow-Bird saw her mother coming fast as the wind.

"My mother is chasing us," said Snow-Bird, "and will catch us before we get away. To save us, I shall use the magic that my father taught me."

Saying the magic words *kunewaas kolos ho hok*, Snow-Bird, fast as light, turned Heat-Man into a hunchbacked old man, Morning Light into the old man's cane, and herself into a log cabin. When her mother arrived, she saw nothing but a hunchbacked old man, with a cane, sitting in front of a log cabin.

The young people were nowhere to be found, so she returned and told her husband what she'd seen.

"Those were our children," said Cold to his wife. "Our daughter has tricked you again. Go after them once more. But this time, do not let her trick you, or I will have to hunt them down myself."

Cold's wife gave chase even faster than before. She knew that if her husband caught the young people, he would kill them out of anger. But if she could bring them back, Cold would be forgiving.

Snow-Bird saw her mother coming in the distance. But Snow-Bird was running out of magic words.

"This trick," she said to Heat-Man, "is the last that I can do. We had better reach the heat country before my father comes howling after us."

Then, saying the magic words *kwad za wad ee nox*, Snow-Bird turned Heat-Man into a pine tree, Morning-Light into a pine cone, and herself into a pine needle. When her mother arrived, she saw nothing but a forest of pine trees, one looking exactly like the next.

The young people were nowhere to be found, so she returned and told her husband what she'd seen.

"One of those pine trees was our children," said Cold to his wife. "Our daughter has tricked you for the last time. I shall go myself—I must hurry, though, or they will reach the country of the heat people."

Cold's wife tried to talk him out of going. She said it was best to let people have their freedom.

"If you go," she said to her husband, "you will kill everything, not only our daughter and grandchild and son-in-law, but also the trees and flowers and animals. Everything you touch will freeze and die."

But Cold was very angry and wouldn't listen to his wife. He started out in fast pursuit, looking for his daughter. He changed into a frigid wind and blew across the lakes and through the forests, freezing everything in sight.

"Now my father is pursuing us," said Snow-Bird, "and there is nothing I can do. If he catches us, he'll kill us with his icy clutch. He is very angry."

They had barely reached the heat country and entered Heat-Man's house when Cold appeared outside. Heat-Man slammed the door and locked it. Cold banged on the front door. Heat-Man wouldn't answer. Cold was furious. He made a snowstorm rage across the heat country. He blew harder and harder. He made all the houses shake. The temperature dropped and the air became too cold to breathe. The heat people, far and wide, grew sick. Heat-Man took his golden staff and tried to stop the cold. He puffed and puffed hot breath. But his staff and breath were powerless against the fury of the icy wind. Pretty soon, Heat-Man took ill. He thought that he would die. Ice began to form inside the house, as well as out. Then Heat-Man remembered his grandmother.

"Grandmother," he cried loudly, "wherever you are, come out, come out and save us. We are dying. Cold is killing us."

His grandmother, who had been visiting her relatives near the middle of the earth, heard his cry. She always carried with her the means for driving off the cold. On her belt, she carried a bag that held the warm wind, called Chinook. She opened up the bag, drew out the Chinook wind, and threw it in the air, saying "Go and warm my people."

The wind flew across the world and, before Cold could turn the heat country into a

solid block of ice, the Chinook began to blow. It blew warmer and warmer until the air was springlike. The ice began to melt and the people recovered. Trees and flowers bloomed again and birdsong filled the air. Cold could see that he was beaten.

"Heat-Man," said Cold, "you have overcome me. You have won the contest. But I cannot bear to lose my daughter. You promised that you would not take her from me. So how do you intend to keep your promise?"

Heat-Man knew that Cold had misbehaved. He knew that Cold deserved to be punished. But Heat-Man also knew that forgiveness is better than revenge.

"If you promise never again to grow angry," said Heat-Man to Cold, "and if you promise to return immediately to the cold country, I will let you come to visit your daughter once a year, but only for a short time.

Cold agreed. Therefore Cold comes once a year to see his daughter. Then it is winter.

And although he sometimes shows his temper, his tantrums never last. Some people think that Heat-Man should have banished Cold forever and not allowed him to return.

But if Heat-Man hadn't kept his promise and granted Cold the right to see his daughter, there would be no winter; and spring and summer, which are valued because they follow from the cold, might not be loved at all.

The Girl and the Dog

Princess Never-Knew-A-Care did not want to marry. Dozens of handsome young men asked her father for her hand, but she rejected them all. Her father may have liked them, but the princess did not. She found each and every one of them far short of what she wanted, lacking in whatever it takes to make a young girl happy.

"Will you not," asked her father, "have Fleet-of-Foot? He runs nearly as fast as the deer that he shoots with his arrow."

"No," murmured Princess Never-Knew-A-Care—and would not say another word. She could not speak. She was sorry for the deer whose heart's blood flowed.

"What, then, of Mighty Archer?" asked her father. "He tracks the black bear through the forest, aims his bow, and lets the arrow fly before the bear has even heard a footstep."

"No," murmured Princess Never-Knew-A-Care—and would not say another word. She was sad for the bear who had to die.

"Then what of Nimble Climber?" asked her father. "He leaps from rock to rock and never falls when hunting mountain goats."

"No," murmured Princess Never-Knew-A-Care—and would not say another word. She pitied the goat whose tallow her father would suck by the fire.

"No, too, for Rolling River?" asked her father. "He sets his traps where the waters run wild and captures the glistening salmon."

"No, too, for him" said Princess Never-Knew-A-Care. She grieved for the sleek, shiny fish, flailing this way and that, caught in the pitiless traps.

"No! Will it always be no?" cried her father, clenching his jaw and shaking his head. "One would think I had asked you to marry a dog."

"I would much rather marry a dog," she replied, "than take one of these men for a husband."

Her father's eyes flashed with fire. Though she looked away, she could still feel his anger. But she refused to change her mind or ask forgiveness for the words that she had spoken. Her father, for his part, kept bringing handsome young men to the underground lodge to court his daughter. Every day, suitors climbed down the ladder to the lodge. But Princess Never-Knew-A-Care rejected them all, saying, "I would rather marry a dog."

Now, one of the many young men who wanted to marry Princess Never-Knew-A-Care lost his temper when he heard what she was saying.

"Bad enough that she's rejected me," he complained. "But to say that she would trade me for a dog—it's more than I can stand. If a dog is what she wants, a dog is what she'll have." And being skilled in magic, he cast a spell upon a dog and sent it whimpering with cold to the underground lodge where Princess Never-Knew-A-Care spent the winter with her people.

Up the ladder came her father, curious to see what child was crying by the entrance to his lodge. But instead of a child, he discovered a poor homeless dog, shivering with cold and looking almost human. The father took him underground and warmed him by the fire. So well behaved and grateful was the dog that the father chose to keep him as his very own.

Little did the father know the dog was charmed. Although by day he was a dog, by night he was a man. As a dog, he was ever the mildest of creatures, nuzzling up to one and all and listening when people told him of their secret cares and wishes. As a man, he was more handsome than the other men and gentler, too, but equally intelligent and strong. And in the form of a man, he appeared every night to Princess Never-Knew-A-Care, and to no one else. The others did not see him. They saw only that the princess went off every evening away from the others. They knew only that she changed her ways. Instead of behaving like a young girl who argued with her father about whom she would or would not marry, she acted like a woman. She acted, in fact, as if she were married.

But who was this man who came to see her every night? Princess Never-Knew-A-Care was bewildered by his comings and his goings. In the morning, when he'd leave her, she never could see him climbing up the ladder that led from the underground lodge to the frozen outdoors. In the evening, when he joined her, she never saw him enter. Who could he be? She wanted more than anything to know; so she made up a trick to find out.

One night, when he came to her room, she hugged him, as she always did. But on her hands there was red ocher, a reddish-yellow clay; and she smeared this clay along his back, without his knowing that she'd done so.

"Yes, hold me tight, my dear," he said, as if he feared to lose her.

But this was the hug that led to his discovery. For when the morning came, Princess Never-Knew-A-Care closely watched as the men climbed the ladder in leaving the lodge. She was looking for a man with red streaks down his back. But one by one, the young men left, and still she was no wiser. Then her father's dog scrambled up the rungs of the ladder, red ocher on his back. Princess Never-Knew-A-Care screamed in horror! So awful was her scream that it killed in the dog whatever had been human and he fled on all fours into the forest. As abruptly as he'd come, he vanished.

To Princess Never-Knew-A-Care, he had been everything. And yet, in truth, he had been nothing but a dog. She cried because she'd lost him but let no one see her tears. No one, in fact, would have known what had happened if the bitter young man who'd enchanted the dog had not spread it about that she'd married a beast, a story she didn't deny.

Her father was ashamed of her, this daughter who had turned away so many fine young men and wasted all her love upon a dog. Chief of the tribe, he determined that in early spring, when the people moved out of their underground lodge and went to the mountains to hunt and dig roots, the princess would be left behind to manage on her own.

How quickly springtime came, and how little joy it brought to Princess Never-Knew-A-Care. In silence she watched as the people made ready to leave her. They packed all their clothing and the pots that they cooked in. They gathered their children together. Last of all, they sprinkled the fire with water. The flames sizzled and spit before dying back into the ashes. Then everyone left. Because they thought that the princess had been cast beneath an evil spell, they were eager to leave her behind.

Only her grandmother showed her some love. Knowing that the others would expect her to be slow because she was so old, the grandmother waited for the rest of the people to go. Then silently she sat beside the princess, sat upon the ground now rich with sweet young grass. Their eyes did not meet, nor their fingers touch; but just their sitting side by side, being there together, was enough for Princess Never-Knew-A-Care.

After a while, the grandmother took from her sleeve the root of a fern that she had hollowed out by sucking. In this root she had hidden a tiny spark of fire, which she gently blew upon until it gave off slender flames. Then she placed the flaming root inside a seashell, and gave the gift of fire to the princess.

"This is for you," the old woman said, "and for the young ones."

"Yes," said Princess Never-Knew-A-Care—and would not say another word. She had known for several months that she'd be giving birth, and in truth, she was afraid.

But she could not show her fear, even to her grandmother. So the princess pretended to be brave. She did not show that she was worried except that her shadow trembled ever so slightly behind her. Had the grandmother seen just a trace of that trembling, she could not have found the strength to go. But facing toward the sun, she saw nothing of the shadow; and thinking she could only be a trouble to the princess, she went to join the others. Thus the princess had no choice but to pass her days alone.

Alone. No one was with her to see what she saw when the dogwood trees flowered and the honeysuckle bloomed. No one was with her to hear what she heard when the raven screeched and beat his huge black wings against the wind. No one was with her to feel what she felt when the rain cooled her eyes and wet her mouth. No one. No one was with her. So when the young ones were born, and there were four of them, it hardly seemed to matter that they weren't boys, but puppies. They were company, and that was enough.

The princess was a mother to the puppies, and a father as well. She gathered them food and prepared it by the fire that she'd gotten from her grandmother. Out of branches of hemlock, she built beside the river a small summer hut to protect them from the weather and from the animals that might have done them harm. When her work, which was not easy, allowed her some rest, she played with the puppies and was happy when they licked her hands or tugged upon her sleeves. And sometimes she'd pretend that they were human, so knowing were their faces. But since pretending is not the same as having, this idea caused her pain; for the children that she wanted were far different from the puppies that she had.

Now about this time the river by the hut was running thick with fish, which the princess meant to catch and store for food throughout the winter that was coming. So one night, when the puppies had fallen asleep, she slipped out of the hut, with a torch to light her way, and made for the bank of the river. Fixing her torch in the thick black mud, she waded out beyond the shore and braved the waves to spear the fish that glistened in the water. And the first night, all was well.

But the second night, no sooner had the princess set her torch beside the river and begun to spear fish than she heard—or thought she heard—the sound of children's voices in the hut where the puppies lay dreaming.

"Ah," she said aloud, though to no one at all, "some children must have lost their way and wandered to this lonely place and found the puppies sleeping by the fire."

Then, taking up her torch, she returned to the hut to greet her visitors. But no one was there except for the puppies, awake and out of breath as if they'd just left off from playing.

"Alas," said she, "I must have heard the water all a-burble and mistaken it for children.

Tomorrow I'll be wiser."

But the next night, too, she heard the sounds of children hard at play; and though she wanted to believe that it was just the water burbling, the rise and fall of voices seemed so real to her that once again she took her torch and went to see what might be seen. And as before she found the puppies wide awake and out of breath.

"Who plays such tricks on me?" she cried. "Ah, well, I won't be fooled again tomorrow." And so the next night when she fished once more and heard the ringing voices, she pretended not to hear.

But she could not close her ears. So teasing was the laughter, so inviting the calls, so lively the sounds, that she felt herself drawn to the hut against her will. This time, though, she left her torch ablaze upon the riverbank, for fear that it gave warning of her coming and thus frightened off the children who appeared to use the hut when she was gone.

Quietly, quietly, ever so secretly, she tiptoed toward the little hemlock hut. And, yes, from inside came the whooping and squealing. Before, at her approach, the sounds had dwindled, then died. But tonight, because no one saw her coming, the voices remained loud upon the wind.

Quietly, quietly, ever so secretly, she peeked between some branches at the back of the hut and saw the impossible. Close to the fire, three bold young boys, with thick black hair and deep bronze skin and lean hard-muscled bodies, rolled and tussled in a boisterous bout of wrestling. Meanwhile, by the window, a fourth boy, just as handsome as the others, stared in the direction of the river, where the blazing torch yet flared beside the water. He was standing watch, acting as a lookout.

Eventually, the wrestling boys gave up their sport and, laughing even now, asked the fourth if he was sure he'd kept his eyes upon the torch.

"I'm sure," he said. "It hasn't moved. She's late tonight. Let's change the watch so I can wrestle, too, before our mother comes."

Mother?! Was it possible? Were these boys, then, her sons? In her surprise, the princess slipped and lost her footing. She fell against the hut's back wall and made a noise that gave the boys a fright.

"There's someone there! Just listen!" cried the children.

But Princess Never-Knew-A-Care was cautious not to make another sound.

She held her breath until the boys began to think that what they'd heard was nothing but the wind.

"What simpletons we are," the boy on watch said boldly. "See, our mother's torch is burning by the river where she fishes. So it can't have been our mother; and no one else has ever come here. We must have heard a branch break from the weight of a raccoon. We're sillier than puppies, my good brothers!" And with that, he kicked a little heap of fur beside his feet.

Dogskins! Four of them were lying there, dropped in a pile, ready for the children to wrap tight around their bodies when they heard their mother coming. So that was the secret of their nightly romps, the disguise by which they altered their appearance. But if the disguise should disappear . . . if Princess Never-Knew-A-Care should take the skins and burn them . . . what would happen to the children then? Would they perish with the skins, or remain forever human?

Princess Never-Knew-A-Care had little time to wonder. The boys expected her return because the hour was so late; and fearing that she might have started home without the torch, they decided to be puppies once again. Why, even at this moment, they were picking up the dogskins, into which they meant to slip. How could she stop them?

Hardly pausing, acting almost without thinking, Princess Never-Knew-A-Care darted to the side of the hut. There she crouched beneath the window and started baying loudly at the moon. The children, all a-wonder, dropped the furs that they were holding and came running to discover what animal was making such a racket. It was just what she had hoped they'd do. For now, as they pushed one another aside, each fighting for a place at the window, the princess flew to the front of the hut, burst in on the children, grabbed the puppy furs from off the floor, and threw them in the fire.

What a wail the boys put up, once they saw what she had done. They nearly leapt into the flames to recover what they'd lost. But seeing that the furs by then were burned beyond repair, they grew terrified and silent.

Princess Never-Knew-A-Care was also terrified. She expected that the boys would disappear before her eyes, that they'd go up in smoke just like the furs, which crackled in the flames. But no, though she waited till the furs fell into ashes, the children did not change. Four boys they had become; four boys they would remain. No longer would she have to live alone.

Now the children bowed their heads and wept for shame to think how cruel a trick they'd played upon their mother. But Princess Never-Knew-A-Care forgave them, saying they had been bewitched. How she hugged them, how she kissed them, these boys who had been puppies just so short a time ago. What did it matter if she'd suffered, now that everything was right? So thought Princess Never-Knew-A-Care; and so she was content.

The boys became her helpers, growing abler as they grew. Soon one could trap deer, and one could trap bear, and one could trap goats, and one could trap fish. And they were all such fine trappers that there was always food enough, and more than food enough, to feed the five of them, the mother and her sons. Even in the deepest part of winter, they had plenty to eat. And always in winter Princess Never-Knew-A-Care would remember her grandmother and wish she could know how the old woman fared.

Thus did it happen one winter, when the wind was unusually cold and food was very hard to find, that Princess Never-Knew-A-Care saw a seagull flying inland. She sighed and murmured soft beneath her breath: "If only you were human, I could beg you to fly to my grandmother's lodge and bring her some food in this bitter time of famine."

And behold, the seagull circled high above her head, dove, and set down beside her feet.

"For the sake of the old one," said the bird, "I will do what you have asked." And taking a fish in his beak, he flew to the place where the grandmother lived. In an underground lodge, he found her warming herself beside the fire and gave her the fish. And not once, but every day, he carried her food, sometimes fish, sometimes game, so that the princess was happy knowing that her grandmother was not hungry.

It wasn't long, however, before the villagers discovered that, by some means or other, the grandmother ate while they did not. Though she pretended that she had no more food than the others, lest they take it away from her, they sometimes caught her chewing by the fire. At first when they asked her what she had in her mouth, they believed her when she said, "Only a bit of cedar bark … to quiet my hunger."

But as the grandmother now would eat hardly a bite from the meager common meals the people shared among themselves, and still she did not starve, everyone began to think she must have found a secret source of food. So they watched her movements closely and discovered that she hid beneath her blanket a supply of game and fish.

Angrily they snatched the blanket from her lap, revealing what she'd hidden. "Wherever did you find such food, when we have none at all?" they cried. "What place produces food that you might share with us?"

"No place at all," she said. "The food I eat is sent to me by Princess Never-Knew-A-Care, the one whom you so long ago deserted. Her sons are now four strong young men who bring her fish from the traps and meat from the hunt."

How the people laughed at her. "A child could tell a better lie," they said. "The princess, if she lives, cannot prosper and have sons. And you, if you insist on being selfish, shall know nothing but our anger." And they prepared to turn her out, to reject her, as before they had rejected the princess.

But the seagull, having heard all this, flew back to tell the princess what had happened. At first she merely shook her head and paced the floor, not knowing what to do. But then a plan occurred to her. She called her sons to gather round.

"My boys," she said. "I must send you on a journey. Take from our cellar as much meat and fat and fish as you can carry. Then put it on your backs, and follow the seagull to a place where he will lead you, and leave what you have carried with the people you will find there."

And without delay, her sons did all that she had asked of them. How astonished were the villagers to see these four young men approach, all loaded down with food. And even more astonished yet were they to learn that their providers were the sons of Princess Never-Knew-A-Care.

"Did we cast her out and wish to do the same to this old woman; and does the Princess now repay us with her kindness?" they exclaimed. And saying this, they wept hot tears for shame. In fact, they cried so long and hard they didn't even notice when the sons of Princess Never-Knew-A-Care slipped off to make their way back home.

All the rest of that long winter, the people ate the food the four young men had brought them. And knowing what they owed the princess, they were ashamed of how much hurt they'd caused her. So when spring arrived, they sent out scouts to scan the country-wide to discover where the princess had been living; and they built a village near to where they found her and invited her to live with them. But she refused to come.

"I have lived so long alone, with just my sons," she said, "that now the only way I know to live is by myself." Her answer hurt the villagers, but well they knew that they deserved her scorn.

Yet anger cannot last without hurting the person who is angry. So to save herself— and also since these people were, in fact, her own—the princess in due season softened and agreed to live among the others. Thus the village once again became a family: the father and the daughter made their peace; the sons took wives and fathered sons themselves; and the princess was surrounded by those who loved her dearly, so that never did she know another care.

The Stolen Appaloosa

Years and years ago, when the world was run by magic, Spirit-Man, a medicine man famous for his power, took a long journey on horseback. After he had traveled over ten mountains, his horse died from exhaustion.

"What I need," he thought, "is a horse that can run forever and will never grow tired."

Sitting on a river bank, he saw in the distance a man riding a horse of a spotted pattern, black and white. It was an Appaloosa, a horse named after the Palouse River. He stared in wonder. He could hardly believe what he was seeing. This horse ran so fast, its feet never touched the ground. It could change direction as quickly as a bee and could soar like a bird.

"I must have that horse," he said to himself; "it covers the earth like lightning." So he used his great magic to make a dust cloud rise from the land. The dust blew in the face of the rider, who failed to hold his breath, and therefore began to choke and cough until his eyes filled up with tears. Blinded by the tears, the rider, whose name was Cawanemux, reined in the horse and drew to a stop right beside Spirit-Man.

The horse, to Spirit-Man's amazement, stood still as stone, not out of breath at all.

"Why are you staring?" asked Cawanemux. "What do you want?"

"Your horse," said the medicine man. "Tell me about your horse."

Cawanemux straightened the mane of his horse and, rubbing the Appaloosa's nose, said, "This horse was born of a marriage between the wind and the loon. Like the wind, he flies everywhere; and like the loon, he swims above and below the water. My Appaloosa," said Cawanemux, "can run around the edge of the earth in two hours. It can smell game behind the mountain and can tell when the winter cold is coming."

"May I ride your horse," asked the medicine man, "just for a minute or two?"

"What is your name?" asked Cawanemux.

"Spirit-Man."

Cawanemux agreed to let him ride his horse and helped Spirit-Man mount the Appaloosa. Pointing to a mountain range about fifty miles away, Cawanemux said, "It will take you about a minute to ride to that range and back. Don't ride any further, because I'm expected home in a few minutes and my village is a hundred miles from here, next to the inland sea."

Spirit-Man lightly touched his heels to the flanks of the horse and immediately the Appaloosa flew off like a streaking comet. Grabbing the mane of the horse, Spirit-Man urged the Appaloosa to outpace the circling sun. In a minute, the horse reached the mountain range, but did not stop. It leapt over the mountain, over marshes and meadows, over gorges, mesas, and buttes, over lakes and rivers and oceans, until it had circled the edge of the earth in two hours. But Spirit-Man did not stop the horse. He rode on and on until he came to his own village, where he hid the horse in a thick wood, so that Cawanemux couldn't find it.

At first, Cawanemux thought the Appaloosa had lost its way. But after waiting until dark, he realized that Spirit-Man had stolen his horse. It was then he began to weep and to swear that even if he had to travel the whole world over, he would find his beloved Appaloosa. When he arrived home, his wife asked why he'd been gone so long. He told her the story of how Spirit-Man had tricked him and had taken his horse away. His wife grew angry, urging him to saddle another horse and set out immediately to look for Spirit-Man.

"Ride from dawn to dark, look in woods and water," she said, "and you will find the Appaloosa. But you must not sleep until you find the horse, otherwise you'll have bad dreams."

Cawanemux took his wife's bay horse from the field where it was grazing, threw a rein over its neck, and rode out of his village in search of Spirit-Man. He knew that the best way to find his horse was not, as his wife advised him, to start looking here and there, in this place and that, because the horse could be hidden in any one of a million places. Instead, he looked up into the sky to see what magic was reflected there in the glassy air. On the second day of his search, he reached the great plains. In the distant sky, he saw a rainbow and falling rain; but there were no clouds. He knew then that Spirit-Man must have called down rain to feed his village garden. So he rode in the direction of the rainbow until he came to the outskirts of Spirit-Man's village. A large field lay before him, a field in bloom with Indian paintbrush, Monk's Hood, and other wildflowers. But before he could cross the field, Spirit-Man saw him in the distance, and magically made a rushing river spring up in the field between Cawanemux and the village, so that Cawanemux couldn't reach him.

What was Cawanemux to do? The bay horse, unlike his Appaloosa, could not leap over a river; and the rushing water would have dashed the horse upon the rocks. The current was too strong for him to swim the river and he couldn't find a narrow place in which to cross, by jumping from one rock to the next. A canoe was too frail to withstand the force of the crashing rapids, and to build a bridge would have taken him several weeks, by which time Spirit-Man would have long been gone. To ride upstream or down, in order to find a place to ford the river, was the only choice he had; so he started downstream, following the course of the current.

Eventually, he came upon a green meadow, with a place narrow enough for him to throw a rope across the river. He fastened the rope around one end of a rock and threw it into a pile of fallen trees on the other bank. The first two times, the rope failed to catch on the trees and pulled loose. The third time, it caught under a log and held fast. He then wrapped the other end of the rope around his waist and, leaving the bay horse behind, waded into the water. Grasping the rope tightly, he let the current sweep him downstream, until the slack in the rope was completely played out. Then, as he had planned, the rope jerked suddenly, yanking him toward the opposite bank. Swimming as hard as he could, he quickly reached the far shore.

But no sooner did he set foot on the other side of the river than Spirit-Man magically caused the green meadow to turn into a sea of quicksand. Stepping into the sand, Cawanemux immediately began to sink: first up to his ankles, and then up to his knees and waist. He struggled, but the sand sucked him ever downward. Struggling only made things worse. The more he tried to free himself, the deeper he sank.

"I must not panic," he thought. "As a child I was taught that if I ever got caught in quicksand, I should lie flat, on either my stomach or my back, and work my way to land."

Inching his fingers to the surface, he slowly freed his arms, which he quickly spread apart, resting them on top of the sand. He then arched his back, freeing it from the sand that held him fast. Little by little, he tilted his body until his back lay upon the sand and his legs began to come free. After about an hour, he had finally positioned his body so that he floated on the surface of the quicksand. He then squirmed, ever so carefully, to the bank of the river, where he tumbled down the bank to the water's edge. Here he lay panting and giving thanks for his escape from the oozing sandy mass.

With all the meadow turned to quicksand, he would have to find another way to capture Spirit-Man. So after his strength had returned, he found his rope, tied one end in a loop, and whistled for the bay horse.

When the horse approached the river's edge, Cawanemux threw the loop of the rope across the river, right around the horse's neck. Then he whistled

for the horse to run. As the bay began to gallop, Cawanemux, who had tightly wrapped the rope around his hands, was pulled across the river. Once on the other side, he unloosed his hands from the rope and called back the horse. Then he mounted the bay and started to ride upstream, toward the mountains, where he hoped to find a place to cross the river, so that he could once again run after Spirit-Man.

Cawanemux rode all day. The flatland gave way to the foothills and the air grew cooler the higher he went. Finally, the foothills became steep gorges and the horse could go no further. Leaving the bay in a grove of aspen trees, he started to climb the rock walls overlooking the river. After several hours of climbing, he saw above him, high up on the mountain, a place where the river narrowed and he could leap across the gorge. But, as it was growing late, he decided to camp and wait until the next day to continue on his journey. He built a fire, ate some huckleberries, and went to sleep. Soon he had a dream. He found himself at the bottom of a lake, trying to reach the surface. From underneath the water, he could see the light of day. But he couldn't hold his breath long enough to reach the air. His lungs began to fill with water; and just at the very moment he thought that he would choke, he woke from his disturbing dream. It was raining, but in the distance the dawn light was beginning to emerge.

He started out immediately, climbing quickly to where the river narrowed; and there he took a running jump and cleared the foaming current down below. Once at the other side of the gorge, he followed the river down the mountain and through the foothills, until he reached the field of wildflowers that bordered on Spirit-Man's village. But as before, Spirit-Man saw him coming in the distance. So he used his magic to turn the middle of the field into a forest full of thick trees and huge boulders.

What was Cawanemux to do? He could hardly squeeze between the trees because they were so close together. One time, when he forced his body sideways through the trees, he nearly got stuck. And when he finally made it through, there in front of him was an enormous boulder, smooth as skin, that he had to shinny up.

"It will take weeks," he thought, "for me to pass through this forest. There must be a better way than squeezing through the trees and climbing over boulders."

Then he remembered what his mother taught him about the squirrel. Instead of running up and down a tree, to get from place to place, the squirrel takes a shortcut, jumping from one treetop to another.

"That's what I will do," he thought. "I'll climb a tree and jump from one limb to the next. I'll go from branch to branch and pass over the boulders down below."

So he shinnied up a tree until he reached those limbs strong enough to hold him. Then he wriggled to the end, as far as it was safe, and dove to the next tree. In this way, he moved from tree to tree, until he had leapfrogged over both the forest and the skin-smooth boulders down below. When he reached the last tree he climbed down, and there before him lay the other side of the wildflower field, the one right next to Spirit-Man's village, which nestled on the plains.

"At last," he said to himself, "I shall reach the village and make Spirit-Man return my Appaloosa."

But before he had taken a dozen steps, the stretch of field that lay before him suddenly turned into a sheet of ice, so slippery he could neither walk nor crawl upon its surface, and so blinding—because the ice acted like a mirror for the sun—he could not see which way to go. What was Cawanemux to do? Spirit-Man had once again used his powerful magic to prevent Cawanemux from reaching him.

"I cannot keep running after Spirit-Man," thought Cawanemux. "He will always be able to stop me with his great medicine. So I, too, must become skilled in the ways of magic."

Lying on his stomach and using his arms to push himself backward, Cawanemux moved off the ice, inch by inch. Then he climbed back across the forest thick with trees and full of boulders, found the bay horse, and rode home to his wife. That night he told her that he'd have to go away again and that she mustn't mind his absence. He explained that he was going to the mountains to purify himself, so that he could learn some magic and therefore not be trapped by the clever tricks of Spirit-Man. When she asked how he would learn the magic, he said that the spirits of the air revealed their secrets to those who fasted, bathed, and prayed. Then she asked if she could help.

"I will need a pair of moccasins," he said, "for living in the mountains and for trying, once again, to find the wily Spirit-Man."

Cawanemux's wife set right to work. She cut the leather and, using rawhide, sewed the moccasins; then she soaked them in animal fat to make the leather soft and waterproof. She told him not to eat while he was on the mountain, otherwise he'd have bad dreams. Cawanemux thanked his wife, said a prayer to his ancestors, and set out walking for the mountain. When he reached the mountain valley where caribou come to graze, he built his sleeping lodge next to a rushing stream and his sweat lodge in a little cave.

For four days, he neither ate nor thought of anything but how to purify himself. On the first day, he placed in the sweat lodge red hot stones that he had baked in fire. Throwing cups of water on the stone, he caused the stones to hiss with steam. Here he sat sweating in the steam until the stones grew cold. Then he plunged into the mountain stream and sat in the freezing waters until the cold stiffened his bones. That night, in order to be learned in the ways of magic, he prayed to the spirits of the air. On the second day, he ran up and down the

mountain paths, in and out between the trees, over and around the boulder fields. When he could run no longer, he bathed in a sacred pond hidden in the Ponderosa pine. Then, in order to be learned in the ways of magic, he prayed to the spirits of the air.

On the third day, he sat in the sweat lodge and afterward he rubbed his body with sandstone to make it clean and hard. Then he jumped into the freezing stream and washed himself with hemlock branches. That night, in order to be learned in the ways of magic, he prayed to the spirits of the air. On the fourth day, he sat in the cold stream water until his body turned to bones and sinews. Then he rubbed nectar on his arms and let the hummingbird suck his blood.

Afterward, in order to be learned in the ways of magic, he prayed to the spirits of the air.

At the end of the fourth day, he felt hungry and ate a handful of huckleberries. That night, he dreamt about his Appaloosa. As he approached the horse, it turned into a bird; and when he tried to reach the bird, it flew away. But then a spirit of the air suddenly appeared. It touched his head and told him that he would, from that day forth, be in command of magic.

The next day, reduced in flesh and feeling very weak, he departed from the mountain and went to live beside the river that runs into the sea. Here he stayed, eating sockeye salmon and camas roots, until his strength returned. Now he was ready to try once again to reach the village of the Spirit-Man. But this time, Cawanemux knew that to avoid Spirit-Man's tricks and find his way to the village, he would have to use magic of his own. Mixing charcoal and tallow, he rubbed them on a cedar stick, and sang the song of the water lily. Immediately a lake appeared, so wide that it stretched from the point where Cawanemux stood to the village of Spirit-Man. Then Cawanemux sang the song of the fish, and a canoe appeared. Painting the prow of the canoe a bright red, Cawanemux took his paddle and set out to cross the lake.

It took him five days to reach Spirit-Man's village. As he neared the shore, the people, seeing his canoe approach, ran and told Spirit-Man.

"A canoe is coming," they said. "Its prow has the face of fire. It will burn us."

Spirit-Man told the villagers not to be afraid. He said that it was all a trick.

"I know who is in the canoe," explained Spirit-Man. "It is Cawanemux. He has come here looking for his horse."

The people in the village were very frightened. They knew that if Cawanemux could make a lake, and make a canoe with a face of fire, he could, if he wanted, do them great harm.

"Spirit-Man," they said, "you must protect us from this medicine man. Give him back his horse. Otherwise he may use his magic to injure us."

When all the villagers began to plead with Spirit-Man, he knew he could no longer keep the horse. But because he was a great medicine man himself, he wanted to see if Cawanemux's magic was stronger than his own. So Spirit-Man changed the Appaloosa into a loon—and then turned himself into a puff of smoke and disappeared in the wind. On reaching the shore, Cawanemux jumped out of his canoe, ran into the village and, going up to a group of people, asked them where Spirit-Man was hiding his horse. The people pointed to a large loon floating on the lake.

"There," they said, "is your horse. Before he disappeared, Spirit-Man turned your Appaloosa into a loon."

Cawanemux did not believe the people. He shook his head in disbelief and searched the village and the woods. But finding nothing, he whistled loudly for his horse. Suddenly the loon on the lake began to neigh. He whistled again, and again the loon neighed. Then Cawanemux knew his horse had been turned into a loon. But when Cawanemux whistled, the loon did not return to shore. It had become a wild bird.

Cawanemux would therefore have to figure out a way to catch it. So he set to work making a net to snare the loon. He wove the net in the shape of a cone, wide at one end and narrow at the other. Hoping to drive the loon into the wide end, he rowed his canoe to the middle of the lake and placed the net just below the surface of the water. Then off he rowed.

But the loon, on nearing the net, stopped, dipped its head in the water, and then darted in the opposite direction.

"The loon can see the net," thought Cawanemux. "I will use a hook to catch the loon."

So he set about making a hook, though not too sharp, that he could drag beneath the water while paddling his canoe. The hook was shaped in such a way that he could catch the loon around its foot. But every time he paddled near the loon, dragging his hook beneath the canoe, the loon fluttered its wings and skittered to another part of the lake.

"The canoe," said Cawanemux to himself, "is frightening off the loon. I will build a decoy and place it on the lake." So he set about making a wooden loon, a decoy that he carved from incense cedar. He painted it to look exactly like a female loon, and then, when the dark of night had fallen, he placed it on the lake.

In the morning, the loon, seeing this handsome decoy, swam after it cautiously. Cawanemux was hidden among the reeds, holding a long string attached to the decoy. As the loon approached, Cawanemux slowly pulled the decoy toward the reeds. Closer, ever closer, came the loon, following the brightly colored decoy. The loon was now almost within his reach.

"Another foot," he thought, "and I'll have caught the loon."

But just as Cawanemux was about to spring, the loon, sensing danger, dove beneath the decoy, plunged to the bottom of the lake, and escaped among the water plants. What was Cawanemux to do?

He took resin of pine and pollen of cedar and rubbed them on his canoe. Then he sang the trout song. Immediately his canoe became a large lake trout. Grabbing hold of its tail, he told the trout to find the loon. The trout, dragging Cawanemux along behind him, swam far out in the lake, found the loon, and began to follow close behind. At first, the loon was frightened by the enormous trout and kept its distance. But after a while, the loon just thought the trout was being playful and, no longer worrying about its size, swam right up beside it. Then Cawanemux let go of the fish's tail and threw his arms around the loon. "You have caught me," said the loon, "but as we are far out in the lake and you cannot swim to shore, you will have to do what I command before I take you safely to the village."

When Cawanemux asked the loon what he would have to do, the loon told him that he would have to hold his breath for minutes at a time, while the loon swam along the bottom of the lake.

"I wish," said Cawanemux, "you would take me to the shore and once again become a horse. After all, haven't I been good to you, trying all this time to catch up with Spirit-Man so that I could bring you home? You should have pity on me."

The loon explained that there was nothing it could do because it was under the spell of Spirit-Man.

"But this is the last obstacle," said the loon, "that Spirit-Man has planted in your way. This is the last test for you to pass."

Cawanemux then climbed on the loon's back, holding fast around his neck.

"I will dive to the bottom of the lake," said the loon. "When you can no longer hold your breath, poke me."

Then the loon put its head in the water and shot off for the bottom, where Cawanemux could see absolutely nothing. All was dark and murky. After one minute, he could no longer hold his breath, so he poked the loon, who surfaced in an instant.

"You must try harder," said the loon, "if you want to get what you desire."

The loon then dived a second time to the bottom of the lake, where Cawanemux could now see the shapes of water plants and fishes swimming by. After two minutes, he could no longer hold his breath, so he poked the loon, who surfaced in an instant.

"Can't you hold your breath any longer?" asked the loon. "You must try harder if you want to get what you desire."

The loon then dived a third time to the bottom of the lake, where Cawanemux saw clearly now, in the sunlight reflected through the water, the different plants and fishes and all the tiny specks of life that live far from human sight. The loon took him all around the lake and Cawanemux never once grew short of breath.

Upon surfacing, the loon said, "You have passed the test. You have learned to hold your breath long enough to see the wonders of the deep. You will therefore have what you desire."

Swimming to the shore, the loon returned Cawanemux to the village. But just as Cawanemux set foot on the land, he found himself magically on horseback along the very river bank where he had first met Spirit-Man. Cawanemux was riding on his Appaloosa, 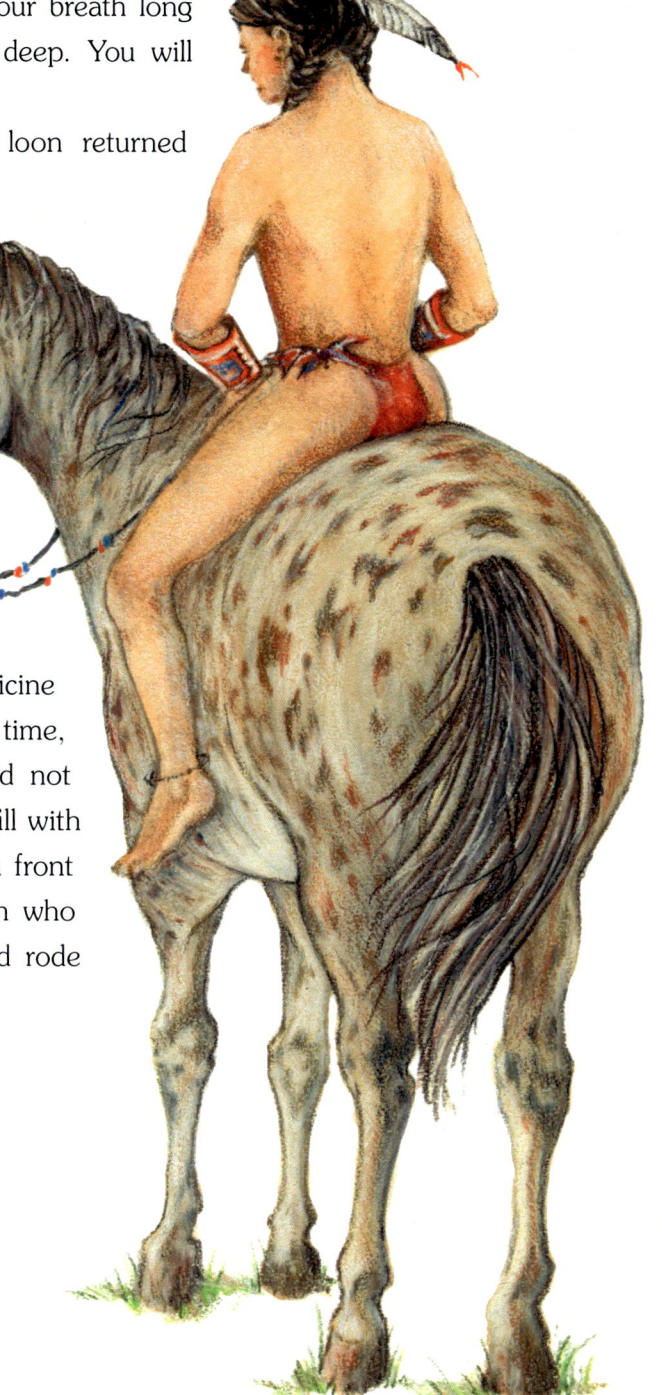 and there in front of him was a medicine man raising a cloud of dust. But this time, Cawanemux held his breath and did not cough, so his eyes did not begin to fill with tears, and he clearly saw the path in front of him. He rode right past this man who strangely looked like Spirit-Man—and rode his Appaloosa home.

The Man Who Journeyed to the Land of the Dead

Long moons ago, in the days before Little Fawn died, Wagisga loved the rain, and the wind, and the sun. Like other Indian braves, he loved to race his pony on the plains, to hide in the cool forest glades, to hunt buffalo, antelope, foxes, and deer. But more than all of this he loved his wife, Little Fawn. She pleased him with her beauty and her gentle grace, and to please her in return was all his care.

When they shivered in the icy winter wind, Little Fawn said, "Never mind. We shall be warm enough when summer comes." But Wagisga would not wait. From pelts of muskrat, mink, and beaver, he made coats to keep her warm.

When springtime rains came dripping through the roof, Little Fawn said, "Let them come. The rains will make the forest bloom." But Wagisga would not hear. From whispering streams he gathered soft reeds, which he placed on the roof of their lodge to keep her dry.

When summer birds ate all their breakfast fruit, Little Fawn said, "Birds must eat, and we still have our bread." But Wagisga would not listen. From his narrow canoe, he speared bright fish to make her morning meal.

When autumn trees wore leaves of gold and flame, Little Fawn said, "Oh, how beautiful they are!" Then Wagisga made her beautiful as well. He gave her silver rings and buckles. He made her gaily beaded moccasins. He gathered many-colored feathers for her hair.

Their lives were passed in happiness and peace. Until quite without warning, on a cold rainy night, Little Fawn died.

Then everything changed. Wagisga no longer raced on his pony, or prowled through the forest. He would not even sit by the fire at night to hear tales of adventure and courage. He would only sit in sadness.

Bright Lightning, the chief of the village, decided that something must be done. But what? He scratched his head. He pulled his ear. He ran his finger up and back across his lower lip. Then he called for Crashing Thunder, the medicine man.

"In your medicine bundle," Bright Lightning said, "you have medicines for every purpose."

"It is true," said Crashing Thunder. "I have roots dug from trees hidden deep in the forest; I have bark scraped from logs black with age."

"And with these scrapings," answered the chief, "I have seen you cure fevers and deafness and many other ills."

"From secret springs," said Crashing Thunder, "I have drawn sweet waters that heal."

"And with these waters," answered the chief, "I have seen you give sight to the blind and strength to the weak."

"From roots, and herbs, and leaves," said Crashing Thunder, "I have mixed magical potions and powerful brews."

"And they have cured rashes and coughs, nightmares and chills," said the chief. "But can they cure Wagisga? He is sick with sorrow at the loss of his wife."

Crashing Thunder shook his head. "There is no medicine to cure a broken heart," he told the chief. But to satisfy Bright Lightning, Crashing Thunder went to Wagisga's lodge.

Once the tidiest home in the village, the lodge was now neglected and bare. The fire was cold in the hearth. The floor was thick with dust. In the darkest corner, Wagisga sat alone. As a sign of his terrible sadness, he had blackened his face with charcoal, which was streaked by bitter tears.

Crashing Thunder lit the fire and swept the floor.

"Wagisga," he said, "be glad that your wife cannot see you. Your sadness would surely break her heart."

For the longest time, Wagisga did not answer. Then, without raising his head or lifting his eyes, he whispered, "You are a powerful medicine man. You have made logs walk. You have made rocks sing. Do you know of a spell that will bring my wife back from the dead?"

"Ghosts may never return to the land of the living," said Crashing Thunder firmly. "And even if they could, we would be wrong to call your wife back. She has only just arrived in the land of the dead."

"Are you sure she is safely there?" Wagisga asked.

"I am certain," replied Crashing Thunder.

"Then I will follow her," Wagisga said, "and bring her home."

"Impossible!" cried Crashing Thunder. Grabbing Wagisga's arm, he whispered, "The path to the land of the dead leads through dark and treacherous valleys, through churning rivers, granite mountains, and pits aglow with fire. No one has ever returned from that journey alive."

"Nevertheless," said Wagisga, "I will go. Just tell me how to get there."

That night, when the village was sleeping, Wagisga set out, following the path that had been mapped for him by Crashing Thunder. At first he almost danced at the thought of

rejoining his wife. But the road was hard, and soon he started to limp. By the end of the day, Wagisga ached in every bone. Pausing to rest, he took a branch and carved a sturdy cane.

"With this," Wagisga thought, "I can support myself on the road that lies ahead."

But the road ahead was littered with stones, and finally Wagisga's cane broke into splinters. Unable to stand any longer, he dropped to his knees and, with great difficulty, slowly crawled along.

"I must not stop," Wagisga thought. "The land of the dead may be just beyond the next turning in the road."

But after many hours, Wagisga had still not come to the end of his journey. Too tired to drag himself another inch, he sank to the ground, and there he fell asleep.

He slept so long that by the time he had awakened he was covered head to foot with fallen leaves. Nearby, he saw an old man patiently watching him. The man had a beard that reached down to his feet, and his face was twisted like a root of an oak.

"So you've come to find your wife," the stranger said.

"How did you know?" asked Wagisga.

"My magic is very powerful," replied the old man. "I know all things. I could help you, if I thought your wife meant all the world, and more, to you."

"I would risk my very life," replied Wagisga, "to find Little Fawn again."

"We shall see if you mean what you say," the old man answered. "Though the danger is great, you must follow this path without fear. I shall meet you at dusk in a lodge by the side of the road. If, my son, you are brave enough to reach it, I will help you find your wife." Then he turned and disappeared.

Was the old man real, or was he nothing but a dream? Wagisga did not know. But deciding to follow the old man's advice, Wagisga started down the trail.

Through the morning and the afternoon the road was easy, and Wagisga traveled fast. "The old man lied," he thought. "There is no danger here." But all at once, a rushing river sprang up at Wagisga's feet. The water crashed round jagged rocks, and seemed to be impassible.

"To get over this river, I'll have to leap," Wagisga thought. "If I fall into the water and drown, I'll be no worse than I am now."

Wagisga took a long running start—and jumped. But the river was much too wide. He was just about to fall into the water, when the wind swept him up into the air and gently blew him to the other side.

"Is it possible?" he wondered. "Have I really crossed the river?" And he turned to look behind him. A desert, dry as dust, stretched as far as his eye could see. The river had disappeared—or maybe only shrunk into the tiny stream that trickled at his feet.

"The old man must have saved me," thought Wagisga. And he was right. The old man admired Wagisga's bravery and, more than that, Wagisga's love for Little Fawn, the love that made him brave. And so the old man helped Wagisga cross the river and filled him full of hope as he continued on his way.

At dusk, Wagisga came to a lodge where the old man sat awaiting him. "You have done well," he told Wagisga. "But there is more that you must do. Refresh yourself. Then continue on the path."

Wagisga washed and ate and slept and, when the morning came, set off again. At first the road was easy, and Wagisga traveled fast. But suddenly a mountain rose before him, smooth as polished glass and strong as granite.

"How can I climb a mountain," Wagisga thought, "without rocks to grab hold of and ledges to stand on? I will never be able to cross this wall of stone."

For many hours, he searched at the foot of the mountain, trying to find a foothold and a place for his hands. At last, he found a crack in which to put his fingers and a narrow ledge on which to place his feet.

"One step is a whole day's work!" Wagisga cried. "I am no closer now to the land of the dead than I was when I set out. I'm afraid it will be months— or maybe years—before I reach the top."

But even as he spoke, Wagisga saw a rocky stair-case open up before him. "The old man has helped me again," Wagisga thought. And he raced up the stair-case like a nimble mountain goat.

At the top, the old man sat awaiting him. "Well done!" he said and clapped Wagisga on the back. "If you have the courage to cross the bridge ahead of you, you'll find yourself in the village of the ghosts."

"At last," Wagisga cried, and ran ahead. The old man hardly had time to shout a warning: "Be careful, Wagisga, the bridge is slippery! And do as I say: be sure to hold your tongue in the land of the dead. If you speak a single word, you will lose your wife forever."

Before the old man's shout had died away, Wagisga was crossing the bridge at breakneck speed. His foot hit a patch of ice, his legs flew out from under him, and Wagisga toppled down toward a roaring pit of fire!

"My life is over now," he thought. But just as the flames began to toast him, a great black bird swooped out of the sky, caught him in its beak, and carried him off to the land of the dead.

By the time they arrived, the sun had already set. Weird shadows flitted wildly through the dark and empty roads. And the voices of the ghosts cried out of the night, "Wagisga will speak before the morning comes. Wagisga will speak and lose his wife."

"It shall not be," Wagisga thought. And he did not say a word.

Through most of the night, the ghosts continued to chant. They banged loud drums and howled fierce cries. They pulled Wagisga's blanket from his back and poked him with sharp sticks. But he would not cry out "Stop!" They knocked him down and dragged him through the roads. But he clenched his teeth and would not make a sound. They pinched him, pushed him, pricked him; but Wagisga was silent.

So the ghosts went way. And Wagisga smiled to think how easily he had succeeded. Soon, he thought, his wife would be his again.

Or would she? Like a terrible nightmare, the ghosts returned, laughing and shouting in Wagisga's ear, "Wagisga will fail. Little Fawn has already forgotten him. Wagisga will fail. Little Fawn has married another."

Wagisga sprang to his feet in a fury. The word "no" was on his tongue and teeth. He opened his mouth to roar with rage, "No, no, not Little Fawn!" But not a whisper would emerge. In the cold and misty night Wagisga, lucky man, had lost his voice.

Now in the east, the sun slowly lit the day, and Wagisga saw that the ghosts had told a lie. On the arm of the kindly old man, Little Fawn came walking towards him. Weeping for joy, Wagisga ran to meet her and closed her in his arms.

"Never before, Wagisga," the old man said, "has anyone been allowed to return from the land of the dead. And from this day forth it will never happen again, because if all the dead returned, the villages would have no room to hold them, and everywhere the land would overflow with hungry people, too many for the earth to feed. But as an everlasting sign to the living that bravery and love are honored by the powers of Life and Death, you and your wife will receive a special blessing. You will leave this place and go back to the village of the living and begin your lives again where you left off." Then he handed Wagisga a bag. "If the ghosts should follow your footsteps and try to capture your wife, open this bag and throw it over your shoulder."

With smiles and thanks, the lovers set off for home. For a day and a night they walked safely, till they came to a forest filled with giant trees. There in the darkness of the woods, at a place where the road ran close to some poison ivy, three ghosts loomed behind them, threatening to pounce. But Wagisga sensed their presence at his back.

Quickly he opened the bag and threw it over his shoulder. What should spill out but ashes: black, sooty ashes, blown back by the wind! Blinded by a storm of swirling soot, the ghosts tripped and fell into the poison ivy while the lovers escaped into the forest. Long after Wagisga and Little Fawn had safely reached their home, the band of ghosts stood crying in the patch of poison ivy, howling that they itched all over.

Raven Finds the Daylight

A long time ago, the world was lit by the moon. There was no daylight. Someone had stolen the sun. So everyone was forced to live by moonlight.

But since the moon is duller than the sun, the world was poorly lit. People were always stubbing their toes on logs and tripping over rocks. Bears never came out of hibernation. And the birds lost their way in the forest. Every day was as dark and as cold as dark winter.

"I can't stand to live without the sun a minute longer," said Mr. Fox, swishing his tail. "No one can see my beautiful coat."

"I can never find my baby chicks," said Mrs. Hen. "They go out to play, and one-two-three they're lost in the night."

"I," said the bald eagle, "am tired of flying into mountains because I can't see where I'm going."

"Enough, enough!" cried Raven. "We must put the light back in the day."

"What can anyone do?" asked Mr. Chipmunk. "No one knows who stole the sun."

"I can fly over the whole world," answered Raven, as he stretched his black shiny wings, "and look for the sun in mesa, mountain, and meadowlands."

"But what if the thief has hidden the sun in a box?" asked Mrs. Rabbit.

Raven thought a moment and said, "The sun is so bright that not even the strongest box can hide all of its rays."

The other animals agreed.

So the next morning, Raven bathed in the cold lake and brushed his feathers with pine cones to make himself sleek for the long flight.

Over the dark patches of forest, the moonlit lakes, and the snow-white mountains flew Raven. He rode the sea breezes and the mountain drafts. Up and down he soared, looking for a beam of sunlight. But all he could see was the cold reflection of the moon. Across lowland meadows and hanging valleys, through mountain gorges and steep ravines he flew, day in and day out, for a year. Until finally, along the edge of the ocean, where the rivers and the salt sea meet, he saw a village of Indian tents. From the largest, the one with a great totem pole in front, a single beam of light shone through a pinhole in the side of the tent.

"That is the tent," said Raven, "of the Chief of the Indians. If he has stolen the sun, how will I get it away from him? He knows all the tricks of Raven."

Swooping down to the village, he settled on top of the totem pole. After checking to see that the coast was clear, he peeked through the pinhole. The great Indian chief was standing. In his hands was a wooden box, fastened with a leather strap.

"In this box," he said to the young Indian braves, seated in a circle around him, "is the wonder of the world. Five years ago, I persuaded the moon and the stars to give me the daylight, which I keep in this box, wrapped in a bearskin. And you must be on your guard always to see that no one takes it from us, especially Raven, who, it is said, has sworn to find the daylight."

Now Raven had a problem. If he pleaded with the Chief that the daylight should be put back in the world, the Chief might grow angry—and put Raven in a cage! Or worse, put Raven in a stew! Raven thought and thought, and finally settled on a plan.

The next day, he went to the pond where the Indians drew their water. When the daughter of the Chief cast her bucket into the pond, Raven, who knew hundreds of tricks and could change into any shape he wanted, turned himself into a tree leaf. As the girl took the bucket from the water, Raven dropped from a tree into the bucket.

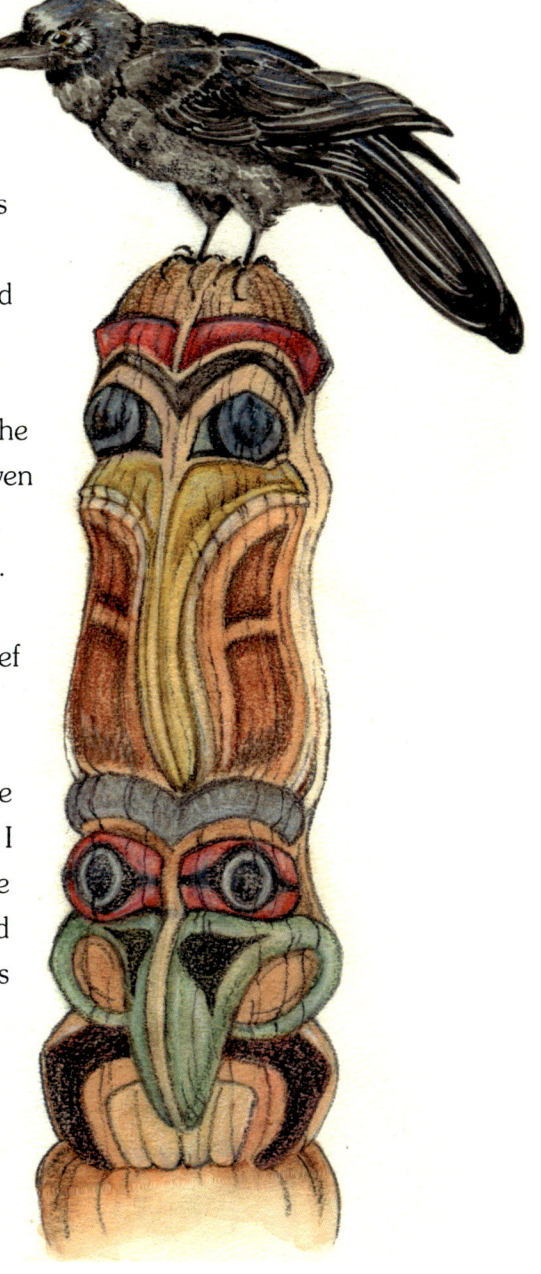

Making her way along the forest path, the girl returned to her father's tent, where a log fire was burning brightly.

"What do you have in the bucket?" asked her father.

"Water … to drink," she answered.

Taking the bucket, the old Chief carried it to the fire and carefully inspected the water. Although Raven had sunk to the bottom, the old Chief was suspicious.

"What is that leaf doing in the water?" he asked.

"Leaf?" repeated the girl. "I see no leaf."

Pointing to the bottom of the bucket, the Chief said, "There! Do you see it now?"

"It's just a birch leaf," said the girl.

"No, my dear," the Chief replied. "It is Raven the trickster. Although I don't know all of his disguises, I know this one." And taking hold of the handle of the bucket, the Chief stepped outside his great tent and spilled the water on the ground, so that Raven was forced to change back into a bird and fly off to a distant tree.

"There he goes," said the Chief, pointing to Raven. "Next time, go to the well and follow the path along the ocean, so that Raven can't fall from a tree into your bucket."

The following day, the girl did as her father suggested. She made her way to the well, which was next to some blackberry bushes in a meadow. As there were no trees in the meadow, Raven could not disguise himself as a leaf. So he turned himself into a blackberry. When the bucket was full, the girl rested it on the ground, in order to catch her breath. In an instant, Raven dropped from the bush into the bucket. Finding the darkest spot in the water, Raven waited to see if his plan would work.

Along the ocean path, through the village, and into her father's tent, the girl carried the bucket of water.

"Have you been careful?" asked the old Chief.

"Yes, father," said the girl.

Lifting the bucket from his daughter's hands, the old Chief tilted his head first one way and then the other. But the log fire had gone out and he could not see clearly in the shadows of the tent.

"Hm," he said.

"Is there something wrong?" asked his daughter.

"Let me just see," said the Chief, as he put the bucket on the ground and went to the back of the tent. A moment later, he returned with the box that held the daylight. Removing the leather straps, he slightly lifted the lid. In an instant, the room was as bright as a snowfield in sunlight.

"Now," said the Chief, "let us look."

Holding the box over the bucket, the Chief peered into the water.

"What is that berry?" asked the Chief.

"Berry?" repeated the girl. "I see no berry in the water."

Pointing to a dark spot, the Chief said. "There. Do you see it now?"

"It's just a blackberry," the girl said.

"No, my dear," said the Chief. "It is Raven the trickster. I know this disguise." And reaching into the water, the Chief grabbed hold of the blackberry.

"I have it!" cried the Chief.

But as he opened his hand to show his daughter, the berry changed into a bird and escaped from the bucket.

"Why," asked the girl, "is Raven trying to play tricks on me?"

"Because," said the Chief, "he wants to find the daylight. From now on, you must get your water from the stream in the rocks, so that Raven can't fall into your bucket from a tree or a bush."

The next day, the girl did as her father commanded. She climbed to the top of the hill that looks out over the ocean. On the other side of the hill was a bare place where a clear stream of water trickled between two rocks. No trees or bushes grew there. Only the wind and the rain and the mountain goats visited this place. Bending over to fill her bucket, the girl did not notice Raven, high in the sky, watching her.

But as the softly running water took a long time to fill the bucket, the girl began to watch some mountain goats playing on the hillside. Raven, floating easily on the ocean breeze, waited until she turned her head. Then he dove straight for the rocks, turning himself, at the last second, into a grain of sand. The girl, hearing the swish of a bird, quickly swung round. Too late. The grain of sand tumbled into the stream, where it was swept into the bucket.

"This time," thought Raven, "I am small enough to hide in the bottom of the bucket and not be seen."

The girl carried the water down the hill, through the meadow, and along the ocean, until she arrived at her father's tent.

"Did you do as I said?" asked the Chief.

"Yes, father. I filled the bucket with pure stream water. Nothing," she said, "fell into the bucket."

Her father smiled and took the bucket from her. Turning it first one way and then another, he looked into the water. But he could see nothing wrong. So he went to the back of the tent and returned with the box that contained the daylight. Holding the box over the bucket, he opened the lid just a crack. Immediately the tent was as light as a summer's day. Closer and closer he looked into the water, until at last he said, "The water is perfectly clear. Now you may drink it."

The young girl reached for her drinking cup, glad that her father had outsmarted Raven; but as she filled her cup, the grain of sand slipped into it.

"For two days," said the girl, "I have been unable to take a sip of water. I am very thirsty." And saying this, she put the cup to her lips and drank all of the water, including the grain of sand.

Once in the girl's stomach, Raven turned himself from a grain of sand into a baby. In due time, the pregnant girl gave birth to Raven, disguised as a baby boy.

At first the little boy played with an Indian rattle, made of deerskin and dried beans. But he soon grew tired of the rattle and cried to play with the box containing the daylight. His mother shook her head and said, "The daylight belongs to your grandfather, the Chief of the Indians, and no one else may have it."

When the boy was a little older, his mother made him a doll. But he soon grew tired of the doll and cried to play with the box containing the daylight. His mother shook her finger and said, "Your grandfather is Chief of the Indians. He has his reasons for imprisoning the daylight. Therefore you must not touch the box."

By the time the little boy was six years old, he was playing with a bow and arrows. But still he cried to play with the box containing the daylight. His mother scolded him and said, "Will you never be still? You know that I cannot give you the box with the daylight. It belongs to your grandfather, the Chief of the Indians."

The child, though, would not be quiet. He cried and cried. At last, the Chief ordered that the child be brought to him. The little boy sat on his grandfather's lap while his mother said to him, "Obey your grandfather. Do whatever he tells you. He is the Chief of the Indians."

Then she left the tent.

The Chief put his arms around the little boy and told him this story.

"When the earth was formed, at the beginning of the world, darkness was all about. Just as I am holding you in my arms, darkness held the world. People lived in caves and lit great fires by which to see and by which to cook their food. One man helped another,

because when people live in darkness, everyone is equal. New beads or moccasins do not matter to people who have trouble seeing. Nor do people notice who has short hair or who has long hair. Every person depends on the other, to keep from getting lost in the darkness.

"Well, after many years of praying for light, the people arose one morning to find the sun in the sky. All about was daylight. It touched the fields and the trees; it reflected in the lakes and the streams; it heated the desert and the ocean sands. Now the world was lit by sun.

"But after the people got used to the daylight, they began to argue about who was the best dressed, the tallest, the richest, the handsomest. They would stare at themselves for hours in the reflection of the ponds. In the clear light of day they threw rocks and shot arrows at one another. Their noisy arguments frightened even the forest animals.

"So one day I asked Mother Moon and Sister Stars to teach me how to catch the sun. They reminded me that the sun comes out of nighttime hiding and brings about the start of day when birdsong rises from the hills. 'The moment birds begin to sing,' they told me, 'the sun sends out a single beam above the border of the world. To catch that beam, you must go to the top of the highest mountain and hide in the snow. There you must wait until the birds of the forest awake and sing their call to daylight. Then, just as the first sunbeam peeks over the edge, throw a wolf skin over the beam and lock it away in a box.' All of which I did. But what Mother Moon and Sister Stars forgot to tell me was that the fog and the rain and the rainbow and loud boisterous thunder were friends of the sun, and they chased me all the way back to the village."

Then the Chief stroked his chin and said, "But I tricked them, too. I told the fog and the rain and the rainbow and loud, boisterous thunder they could have back the sun if they would silently sit in my tepee, wrapped up in the smoke of the fire. Then I quickly extinguished the fire, caught the last puffs of smoke, which held the fog and the rain and the rainbow and loud boisterous thunder, and put them all in different boxes. And though I sometimes let the fog and the rain and the rainbow and loud boisterous thunder peek out, I always keep the sun locked up, except in an emergency."

The child pleaded with his grandfather to give him the box with the daylight, and swore that he'd be ever so careful.

"Then," said the Chief, "I will give you the box that contains the daylight." He put the child down and went to the back of his tent. When he returned, he said, "Here is the wooden box with the daylight."

The child took the box and sat down with it in a far corner of the tent. After a few minutes, he said, "Grandfather, why doesn't the light leak out of the box?"

"Because I keep it wrapped in a bearskin," replied his grandfather.

A few minutes later, the child said, "Grandfather, I wish to play outside with the box."

"All right," said the Chief, "but remember: you are not to remove the bearskin and open it."

As soon as the child was outside, he ran into the woods, removed the bearskin, and opened the box. But instead of the day being lit by light, a great fog came over the world. The child quickly ran back to his grandfather's tent.

"You were warned," said the Chief, "not to remove the bearskin and open the box. But you did not listen. Now you have let loose the fog."

"Please don't be angry, Grandfather," said the child. "I tripped, and the box fell from my hands, causing the bearskin and box to open."

"I was testing you," said the Chief. "Next time you must listen to me."

Then the Chief went to the back of the tent and returned with a wooden box wrapped in a bearskin. "Here," said the Chief, "is the box with the daylight."

The child took the box and went to play in a far corner of the tent. After a minute or two, he said, "Grandfather, may I play with the box outside?"

"Yes," said the Chief, "if you remember not to remove the bearskin and open the box."

"I'll remember," said the child, as he ran outside, heading straight for the woods.

On a grassy spot, he sat down. But this time, the child, who of course was Raven in disguise, had barely thrown off the bearskin and raised the lid of the box, when immediately he heard the sound of thunder. Then rain began to fall. Shutting the box quickly and wrapping it in the bearskin, the child ran back to his grandfather, and said, "I do not like this box. I want the one that contains the daylight."

The Chief listened to the child and then asked, "What makes you think that the box I gave you does not contain the daylight?"

"Well," said the child, "a raven flew down from a tree and grabbed the bearskin holding the box. But as the raven tried to fly off, the box fell out of the bearskin. When it hit the ground, the lid opened—just a crack."

"It's lucky," said the Chief, "that the lid did not open more than a crack. Otherwise we might have been flooded. You see," explained the Chief, "the box I gave you held the thunder and rain."

"Please, grandfather," said the child, "may I have the box that holds the daylight?"

The Chief walked into the dark at the back of his tent and returned with a wooden box wrapped in a bearskin. "This," said the Chief, "is the box that contains the daylight."

The child took it and sat on the ground. In a short while, he asked his grandfather if he could take the box outside. When his grandfather said he could, the child again ran into

the forest. But this time, he went to a small cave in the hillside. Crawling through the narrow opening, he pushed a rock against the entrance so that nothing could leave or enter the cave. Then the child removed the bearskin and opened the box—just a bit. In a moment, the cave was as bright with color as the autumn trees and the flowers of May. The box contained the rainbow.

Once again the Chief had been testing his grandson.

Removing the rock from the opening of the cave, the child crawled out and ran home. Handing the box to his grandfather, the child said, "Thank you, Grandfather, for letting me play with the box that contains the daylight. I know how valuable the daylight is. So I was very careful not to open the box. I hope now, Grandfather, that you are proud of me."

The Chief, turning to the boy's mother, said, "I am very proud of my grandson. He obeys my commands and is to be trusted in all things."

Then the Chief went off to take a nap. While he was asleep, the child asked his mother for the box containing the daylight. At first she refused, saying that she would have to wait until the Chief awoke. The child cried:

"Grandfather trusts me, why won't you?"

The mother was ashamed. So she gave the child a wooden box wrapped in a bearskin. "Here," she said, "is the daylight. Do not stray into the forest. Play close to the tent, where I can see you."

The child sat down outside the Chief's tent. By rolling the box in front of him, a foot at a time, he was able to move slowly from the tent to the forest. When the child had almost reached the trees, his mother called to him to come back.

"You have gone too far," she cried.

At that moment, Raven changed into a bird and flew off with the box wrapped in a bearskin. Flying higher and higher, Raven raced across the sky, mile after mile, day after day, until, weak with hunger, he landed in a cranberry bog, where three women were picking berries.

"If you will give me some berries," said Raven, "I will put the daylight back in the day."

"How can you do that?" asked the first woman.

"You're just trying to trick us," said the second.

"I don't believe you," said the third.

Raven removed the bearskin and put the wooden box on a flat rock. But Raven was worried. Did he have the right box this time? Or had he been tricked once again? Because if he didn't have the right box, he'd probably never get another chance to recover the daylight. Holding his breath, Raven lifted the lid of the box a tiny bit . . . and suddenly, all across the ocean and forest, as far as the eye could see, it was twilight. The women were so excited, they gave him some berries. A crowd of people came running, all drawn to the twilight. And they, too, gave Raven berries. In appreciation, Raven opened the box all the way, causing the daylight to shine, brilliant and gold, throughout the world—all the time.

But pretty soon, the people grew tired of having golden daylight all the time, morning, noon, and night. So Raven said to the light:

"Since I have set you free, do me this favor: half the time be dark, and half the time be light, as it was at the beginning of the world."

And this is how Raven restored night and day.

ABOUT THE AUTHORS

Paul M. Levitt

Paul M. Levitt is Professor of English at the University of Colorado at Boulder.

His courses range from modern drama to the gangster novel. He has written plays, novels, children's tales, medical books for the general public, and scholarly works on theater subjects. For recreation, he likes to play tennis, walk, and travel.

Elissa S. Guralnick

Elissa S. Guralnick is Professor of English and a faculty member in the College of Music at the University of Colorado at Boulder. In her scholarly work, she has written about drama, poetry, and song. In addition, she is an avid amateur pianist.

Together with Douglas A. Burger, Levitt and Guralnick are co-authors of two imaginative, highly acclaimed, and lushly illustrated vocabulary builders for children: *The Weighty Word Book*, illustrated by Janet Stevens, and *Weighty Words, Too*, illustrated by Katherine Karcz.

ABOUT THE ILLUSTRATOR

Carolynn Roche

Carolynn Roche holds a Bachelor of Fine Arts from the University of Colorado, Boulder.

Since 1980, her watercolor work has been shown in the Rocky Mountain area. Her particular interest in the Native American art and culture of the western United States has provided background for her illustrations published in children's books. The illustrations for *Raven* were done in watercolor and colored pencils on paper.

Carolynn continues to live an artful life in her old adobe home in Pueblo, Colorado, where she now produces art for her own pleasure.